BREAKING BEDROCK

THE BEDROCK SERIES | BOOK TWO

BRITNEY KING

WWW.BRITNEYKING.COM

ALSO BY BRITNEY KING

Bedrock

Beyond Bedrock

The Social Affair

Water Under The Bridge

Dead In The Water

Come Hell or High Water

Around The Bend

Somewhere With You

Anywhere With You

BREAKING BEDROCK

BRITNEY KING

COPYRIGHT

Hot Banana Press
Front Cover Design by Lisa Wilson
Back Cover Design by Britney King
Cover Image by Sebastian Kullas
Copy Editing by TW Manuscript Services
Proofread by Proofreading by the Page

First Edition: 2013
ISBN: 978-0-9892184-7-4 (Paperback)
ISBN: 978-0-9892184-2-9 (All E-Books)
britneyking.com

For the William in my life,
we should all be so lucky . . .

CHAPTER ONE

This is a story about truth, to be sure. Who's truth, well, that's for you to decide. More than that, it's about good versus evil; it's about winning and losing. It's about the darkness that lives inside each of us. However, strip it all down and you'll find underneath, it's a love story. But then, really, aren't they all?

It is my belief that love is mostly about showing up. It's about showing up in the good times and especially in the bad. It's about being there, and continuing to be there, particularly when the going gets tough. Because that's the thing about love, isn't it? The going *always* gets tough. But, if you can manage to dig your heels in, day in and day out, no matter what life brings, I think you'll find that you might just come out on top. In time, you might come to find that while love and what you thought you knew of it, may in fact, look very different than you'd imagined, it's there nonetheless. Even when it's dark and unpredictable. I find, all the best things are.

~

Addison Greyer pulled the sweatshirt over her head, stuffed her keys and phone in the pocket, grabbed her pepper spray and headed out for the run she so desperately needed. It was a cold, dreary morning, the kind where the cold settles in your bones until it hurts. Gripping the pepper spray tightly, she rounded her driveway, taking off in full sprint, pushing herself harder and faster than she had in some time. Although her eyes stung and her lungs burned, Addison knew better than to give in. She knew better than to stop. Not today. Today there was no stopping. Today was about pushing through the pain, today was about getting to the other side, only to find there is no other side. It didn't matter. Today she would run and run and run until she couldn't.

She would run and she would let her mind drift back and forth over the past few months as though searching for a clue, any tiny shred of evidence that may have simply been overlooked. She'd played out this scenario hundreds of times, hoping that she could find something she'd overlooked, a missing piece that if found, would make everything clear. She needed to run. But, she also needed things to make sense.

It wasn't unusual that William Hartman weighed heavily on Addison's mind, and today was certainly no different. Unfortunately, the situation had become significantly worse over the past twenty-four hours, and no matter what she did or how she tried to keep herself busy, she couldn't stop her thoughts from returning to the letter. Her mind replayed the words over and over. She'd memorized them. They'd etched their way into her soul, just like the cold weighed on her bones, only worse. She recalled now, her breath heaving against the cold, how she'd traced her finger around the smooth edges of her finest stationery and then carefully tucked it in the envelope. She'd taken the letter out again just to run her fingers over it one last time as though maybe, just maybe, she could tuck a little bit of herself in with it. She closed her eyes and silently prayed that the letter's recipient might feel her, that forgiveness might be nestled between the lines. She even entertained the idea that if she were to concentrate hard enough, perhaps she might undo what she'd done—how quickly she'd emailed the courier and scheduled for a pick-up before calling to cancel, only to finally call back and schedule once more.

Still, no matter how her heart struggled against what she'd done, her mind knew it was the right thing to do. Addison hadn't been able to forgive herself after what would be forever dubbed "the disastrous Christmas-tree event." It had been that night as she pressed her head to the smooth cold tile of her bathroom floor, tears streaming silently down her face, that she finally understood what it was she needed to do. It was time she let him go, once and for all. She wasn't good for him. He wasn't good for her. At least not in any of the ways that mattered, when it came right down to it. That much was clear. Asking him to wait for her wasn't fair. Asking him to be something he wasn't would never work. Her life was a complete and utter mess. There wasn't room for anything else, certainly not love and all of its glorious chaos.

For starters, Scott Hammons, the man who had kidnapped and tortured her, had been arraigned, pleading not guilty, and was out on bail. He'd somehow managed to retain counsel who was able to convince a judge to allow him a pre-trial release after agreeing to a strict no-contact order, 24/7 electronic monitoring, and of course, after having posted a hefty amount of bail money. None of that mattered to Addison. No restraining order and certainly no ankle bracelet was enough to make her feel safe. She'd seen what Scott Hammons was capable of, not to mention the look in his eye at the arraignment, full of contempt. She knew he wasn't finished with her, not by a long shot. But if that weren't enough, her husband was blackmailing her to stay in a marriage that they both knew deep down, whether he wanted to admit it or not, was broken beyond repair.

Suffice it to say, not only was her life in turmoil but it was certainly no place to let love walk in. The next few months would be precarious, at least until the preliminary hearing, and quite frankly, Addison realized, there was no room for anything more than survival. Given the thoughts of Scott Hammons and what she might have to do to put an end to the situation, once and for all, Addison pushed herself harder. She embraced the cold, welcomed the pain, feeling each step as her feet pounded the payment. The faster she ran, the more the words she'd written played in her mind, words that would never, could never, be enough.

Panting hard and slightly dizzy, Addison was trying to recall whether or not she'd eaten anything that morning when a sudden movement up ahead caught her eye, causing her to stop abruptly in her tracks. After focusing in and realizing she recognized the car, Addison sighed and braced herself, knowing exactly what was waiting for her down the road.

~

WILLIAM HARTMAN TURNED THE UNASSUMING ENVELOPE OVER in his hands and considered the weight of it. No one sent letters like this anymore, and this one felt familiar, classy; important. He didn't open his own mail and whoever had sent this understood that, which meant that it could only have come from a small pool of senders. Opening it, he admired the stationery, realizing exactly who it was from and what it would say. William sank back in his chair, ran his fingers through his hair and proceeded to take it all in.

Dear William,

I've wanted so many times to call over the past week, but with the trial coming up, the attorneys have instructed me not to have any contact with you. In addition, it's very plausible that you have no interest in hearing from me today or any other day for that matter. But I want to tell you that I'm sorry, William. I am so very sorry for so many things. I'm sorry for making the decisions that I did, I'm sorry for dragging you into the chaos that is my life, I'm sorry that you saw what you did the other night in the park, and I will be forever sorry that I didn't have the strength in that moment to do and say all the things I should have.

There is one thing, however, that I am not sorry for: falling in love with you. I want you to know that I would give just about anything to be where you are, to be in a different time and a different place. And I want you to know, for what it's worth, that I wish I could take back the way things turned out in the park. But I can't. And the truth is, what happened has given me the clarity to understand what I need to do from here.

I need to move forward with my life, William. I need to move forward with the way things really are, the way they currently stand, not how I wish they were. I have to beat Scott Hammons in this trial. I need to prove to him, and everyone else, that what he did to me was real, that I'm *not* what or who they're going to say I am. I need to know that my children are safe and secure and I need them to know that their mother loves them and would do ANYTHING for them. For the time being, that means I need to stay in my marriage, and for what it's worth, I can't very well do that with one foot out the door. And more importantly, I cannot very well do that and at the same time be hopelessly in love with you.

I have to let go for good this time. The irony here is that it's fairly likely that you already have and that I really don't have to say any of this at all. Honestly, if we're facing facts here, it appears that we've both let go. But so long as neither of us says it out loud, it can't be real, can it? I guess that's why I felt I needed to say it.

Again, I'm sorry, William. I am sorry I hurt you. I'm sorry to have been just one more person in your life to let you down. And while I regret the aftermath, I do not, for one second, regret anything that happened between us. I have been a better person for it.

I hope for you the very best that life has to offer; and I want to thank you. Thank you for loving me. But most of all, thank you for showing me a side to love I'd never known before: the best side.

A world of love,
Addison

WILLIAM METICULOUSLY PLACED THE NOTE BACK IN ITS envelope. He'd been right about one thing. It was classy; that was for sure. Suddenly needing to let off steam, he laced his running shoes and headed downstairs to the gym but not before placing a phone call that could no longer be delayed. Apparently, Addison Greyer had forgotten who she was dealing with. Too bad for her, William had just decided he was finished playing nice. This time, he wasn't fighting fair.

CHAPTER TWO

Addison walked slowly toward the woman who had once been her boss. Leaning against the car driven by a driver Addison didn't recognize, Sondra Sheehan was dressed to the nines just as she always was. It seemed motherhood hadn't slowed her down in the least, she thought, stopping a good five feet away. She simply stared. *It's better to wait, than to lay your cards on the table before the dealing is done.*

"What in the hell has gotten into you, Addison?" Sondra asked, closing the gap between them. "You don't return my calls, you don't answer your emails, and quite frankly, you look like shit."

Addison frowned. She wasn't sure how one was supposed to look after a long run, but surely not stunning.

"It really doesn't surprise me that I had to drive all the way over to this godforsaken place, this suburban hellhole," Sondra added. She tilted her head and crossed her arms.

Addison shifted from foot to foot. She stared down at the pavement.

"Well," Sondra demanded. "Are you going to explain it to

me or not? Why is it too much to ask for some simple decency?"

Addison slid her sweaty hands down her workout pants before straightening up and meeting Sondra's gaze. "Well, hello to you, too."

"This isn't a joke. We need to talk, Addison."

Addison turned and walked toward her house. She shrugged and threw up her hands. "Who's joking?"

Sondra's heels clicked on the walkway as she tried to keep up. "I need you to listen to me, and I mean *really* listen."

Addison unlocked the front door and ushered Sondra in. She closed it, carefully making sure to lock each of the three deadbolts. Then she leaned back against the wall, folding her arms. The dizzy feeling hadn't quite subsided. "Ok," she said, gesturing toward the living room. "You have my full attention."

Sondra sighed and followed her. "Look," she said. "You know me...I like to cut right to the chase."

Addison raised her brow. "As do I..."

Sondra inhaled and let her breath out slowly. "Alright. I need you to come back to work."

Addison scoffed. Sondra continued. "The firm needs you. The clients love you, and, quite frankly we've had a few who have bailed on us in your absence."

"Bullshit." Addison said.

Sondra shifted. "Excuse me?"

"I don't buy it. Sure, maybe *you* want me to come back. I just don't buy your reasoning; that's all."

Sondra smirked. "You know, Addison, there's a reason I've always liked you."

She didn't respond but instead plopped down on the sofa, sat back, and waited for what she knew was coming.

"You don't take anything at face value. And I appreciate

that. I hope in return you can appreciate my keen eye for detail."

Addison narrowed her gaze. "And…"

"The truth is the firm does need you and the clients do love you. But what I really need is for William Hartman to see that you're back."

And there it was. *Bingo.*

She almost smiled. "Not a chance."

"Addison, he's threatening to shut us down. We both know he's not pleased with me. After everything that happened, well, I think if he could see that you've forgiven me and that you are willing to give this whole thing another shot, then perhaps he would, too."

Addison sighed. "I have forgiven you."

"Have you, though?" Sondra questioned. She perched herself on the armrest of Addison's favorite oversized chair.

"Yes, I have."

"Well, then, what other reason could there be for you not coming back to the agency? Look, I'm not asking you to work for me as a Domme. I understand that ship has sailed. But the agency, it does need you. And forgive me if I'm being presumptuous," she said, gesturing around the living room. "But I think you need *it* a little, too."

Addison sucked in her bottom lip. "First, you insult my appearance and now you're insulting my home. Why would I want to work for you? For anyone like that?"

"Because deep down you know what I'm saying, even if it's worded rather harshly, is true."

Damn it. That woman always knew exactly how to hook her. Addison considered Sondra's proposal, although she'd known her answer the moment she'd spotted the car. "Fine," she said. "I'll come back. Give me a week to sort things out here, and I want a new contract—with shorter hours and more pay." Addison allowed the words to slip right off of her tongue, full-well knowing she shouldn't be agreeing to what she was agreeing to, not in a million years.

But Sondra Sheehan had been right about one thing. Addison did need *it*. The trouble was she couldn't discern just which *it* she was referring to.

~

WILLIAM GESTURED TOWARD HIS CELL AND STEPPED OUT OF the meeting upon seeing the number on the display.

Clearing his throat, he answered. "Well?"

"You've won, William, all right? She agreed to come back," Sondra huffed. "But I swear if you ever blackmail me again it will be the end of any kind of relationship we have."

"Just like that?" William grinned from ear to ear. *Obviously, he'd underestimated Sondra.*

"No, of course not 'just like that.' She's a pain in the ass, and she had a list of demands, which I fully expect Hartman Industries will meet. What I mean to say is this is going to be your budgeting issue, not ours."

He pinched the bridge of his nose and exhaled long and slow. "I don't see that being a problem, but seriously? She agreed? I assume that you left my name out of it as per my request…"

Sondra rolled her eyes. "Don't flatter yourself so much, William. It's not about you. She needs the money. Now, I have *real* business matters to attend to, so if you'll excuse me . . ."

William tugged at his tie and then stared at his shoes, cutting her off. "Nice work," he said. "See you at six."

"About that—don't test me, William. As you know, trust is at the heart of every relationship. I advise you not to taint ours. Clearly, I must be missing something. I just don't see what's so important about this girl, or why you'd be willing to put so much on the line. Come to think of it, I may have to ask that you enlighten me during our session. Is that what you want?"

William smiled. "Whatever it takes."

CHAPTER THREE

Addison reached for the door in a hurry; trying to beat the downpour she knew was coming. She ducked inside the coffee shop, stopping just inside the entrance, where she shook the mist from her dress and took it all in. *She'd missed this.* Addison loved the hustle and bustle of the crowd, the laughter and the whispers, but most of all she loved the variety of aromas. This particular coffee shop felt like home to her. It was where she and her best friend Jessica had met weekly every Monday morning since college. In the early days, it was just for a quick cup and a few words here and there on Addison's way to work and after Jess had finished her morning workout. But as time went on and babies came, they'd each wheel in their strollers and sometimes sit for hours in between their kids' nap and snack schedules. There were many weeks where that Monday coffee date was one of the few things Addison looked forward to, but that wasn't the case now, not today.

She noticed Jess first sitting in the corner in "their spot." Staring out the window as though searching for something,

Addison couldn't help but smile. Her friend looked more beautiful than ever. While Addison's life was falling apart, Jessica was thriving. This had undoubtedly taken a toll on their friendship, even if it was an unspoken one. The only person harder on Addison than she was on herself was Jess. She'd always loved this about their relationship, the fact that Jessica pushed her to be better. She never let Addison off the hook, but her advice was always delivered with love, until their last conversation several months ago in her hospital room. The two hadn't spoken since then, well, not in the ways that mattered. Addison took a deep breath in and held it. *It's now or never*, she thought letting the air out slowly. She walked over to the table.

"Jess," Addison whispered.

Looking up, Jess smiled as Addison gripped her tightly. Addison pulled back a bit, noticing again how good her friend looked. All at once she realized just how much she'd missed her.

"Here," Jess said. "I ordered for you." She pushed the cup across the table.

Addison lifted the hot cup and tilted it in her friend's direction as though to say cheers. "Thank you."

"Look, Addison... I don't even know where to start..." Jess said, sipping her coffee. "Mainly, I just want to apologize for everything I said. It wasn't my place, and I realize that."

Addison smirked. "Oh well, when has that ever stopped you before?"

"I'm serious," Jess warned. "Just hear me out, please. I need to say this... I'm sorry for how hard I came down on you before. It's just . . . It's just that— I realized how close I came to losing you—how everyone almost lost you. However—I do stand by the fact that you made some very, VERY stupid choices, but I shouldn't have allowed my anger, or more accurately my fear, to get in the way of being there for you. And, for that, I'm sorry."

Addison took a long sip, letting the smooth hot liquid run down her throat. "I know, Jess. But everything you said was true. And the truth is, I let you down. I let a lot of people down." Feeling tears well up, Addison stopped herself from saying anything further.

Always one to know the right thing to say, Jess changed the subject. "How are the boys?"

"They're good. Thankfully, they really don't seem to notice anything is out of the ordinary."

"And Patrick?"

"Patrick is, uh, you know, Patrick."

"Addison?"

"Yeah?"

Jess leaned in close, crossing her arms on the table. "This is me you're talking to."

"I know."

"So…tell me everything, and start from the beginning. Why did you sleep with him?" Jess asked raising her brow. "How did it start? And most importantly, why in the hell did you keep it all from me? I feel like I don't even know you."

"Sometimes it feels as if I don't even know myself," Addison sighed.

Not letting her off the hook, Jess pressed on. "Okay, so, tell me. I want to hear it all."

"Come on, Jess. You know the story. The media's plastered it everywhere."

Jess shook her head. "I don't give a fuck what the media says. I want to hear it from you."

Addison took a deep breath in, let it out, and then sat up a little straighter. "Ok…well… I didn't mean for any of this to happen. It just kind of did. And I know how cliché that sounds," she shrugged. "But it's the truth."

"You didn't answer my question… How did it start?"

"In the elevator. The day of my job interview actually."

Jess swallowed. Addison went on. "I made a mistake that day in the elevator. I guess that's where it started. It was so out of character for me to have sex with someone I didn't even know. And I wouldn't have, had I not been half-drunk. But the really odd thing is I felt as though I did know him, Jess. There was something in his eyes I saw . . . I can't exactly explain it, but there was something I recognized. And I realized right then and there, that I wanted whatever *that* thing was. So— without even thinking really—I just told myself what the hell? I just let go and went with it. I don't know why. For once, I guess I just listened to what my heart was telling me and drowned out the voice in my head. And you know what, Jess? That's how it is with him. I just feel. It's different than anything I've ever experienced. I can't explain it . . ."

Jess reached for Addison's hand and squeezed. "Oh, honey, you're in so much trouble."

Addison waved her off. "No, I ended it," she said. "It's done."

Jess tossed her head back and laughed before her face grew serious again. "For who?"

Addison pondered her question for a moment before speaking. "For everyone. I need to focus on my family, on the trial, and of course, on work."

"And Patrick? Wait," Jess said, doing a double take. "You're going back to work? So soon?"

"I have to. I mean . . . I need the work, Jess. Sitting around that house, I'm losing my mind."

"But do you think it's really a good idea? And what about Patrick?" she demanded. "You never answered me."

Addison looked away at the mention of her husband's name. She stared out the window, watching the rain as it hit the pavement. "Yeah, actually, I do think it's a good idea. I know you won't understand but—"

Jess frowned. "Addison?"

Addison turned, looking her friend straight in the eye. "I don't know what you want me to say, Jess. Patrick's blackmailing me to stay in a marriage I don't want to be in. He's threatening to take the kids if I leave. Does it even matter that we're strangers sharing a bed, a home, and a life? Should I stay in this marriage anyway?"

"That's not what— "

Addison cut her off. "I know. I know what you're going to say. And I don't even know where to start to unravel the mess that it is. Quite honestly, I'm just trying to get through each day alive and stay sane in the process. Aside from that and my children, that's about as much as I can focus on at the moment."

Jess nodded toward the door. "Is that why there are men in suits following you? Watching your every move?"

Addison sighed and spoke without looking in their direction. "Them... they're security. Employees of William's. I ignore them mostly. I've told him, not that we've spoken, but I've told him before it's not necessary. Although . . . I guess . . . in some ways, it's nice knowing they're there."

"Because you know it's not over if he cares enough to send them?"

Addison narrowed her eyes. "No. Because I'm not sure that the threat of Scott Hammons is over. I think he's going to try and finish what he started."

Jess shifted. "Was he really a client, Addison? And, if so, why in the fuck would you get mixed up in something like that?"

"Was who a client?" Addison replied, fidgeting.

Jess scoffed and shifted once again. "Seriously, Addison! Is this *that* bad? So bad that you don't even know which one of them I'm talking about?"

Addison downed the last of her coffee and slammed her cup down on the table. "I don't know, Jess. It seems to me that just like everyone else, you believe the lies the media is feeding you."

Jess shook her head and looked away. "I don't know what to believe."

"Scott Hammons tried to kill me. He kidnapped and beat me. No, he wasn't a client. He . . . He just has something against William, and I happened to get caught in the cross-fire. I was in the wrong place at the wrong time; that's all."

Jess rolled her eyes. "You don't say."

Addison threw her head back, laughing maniacally. "Ha. Well, that's nice. If my best friend doesn't even believe me, then *who* will?"

"No one . . . if you go back to that job."

"I'm not working as a Domme anymore if that's what you're suggesting."

Jess folded her arms across her chest. "Isn't it one and the same?"

Addison reached for her purse and gathered her things. "Look, Jessica, I'm trying here. I'm really trying. I'm not pretending that I've made the best choices lately, but I have to go back to work. I'm not like you. Some of us do have to work for a living."

Jessica grabbed Addison's forearm as she stood to leave. "I know you're not like me, Addison. I know you're hurting. Anyone can see that. And I wanna help you, sweetie. I love you," she said, squeezing. "But you have to let me in, okay?"

Addison sank back in her chair, the desperation in her best friend's eyes dissolving any anger she'd had. She let it all pour out in a hushed whisper, as though maybe if barely audible, what she was saying wouldn't be true. "I didn't mean to fall in love with him, Jess. And now I can't make it stop. I can't just wish it away. You're right. It hurts like hell, and I don't know what to do about it. Sure, I can double down in my marriage and forget about him. That's the right thing to do; I know it."

"Addison..."

"But my heart, Jess, it won't let me. It's futile, so I ended it because I know it's what's best for everyone. My heart is broken, Jess. And I don't think anything will ever or can *ever* be the same. I love him . . ."

"So, what are you going to do?"

Addison let the tears spill over and brushed them with the back of her hand. "I don't know."

Jess took both of Addison's hands in hers. "Oh, honey, you'll figure it out. I know you."

"We'll see."

Jess glanced at her watch and frowned. "Shit. I've gotta run. But what do you say... same time, same place, next week?"

"Jess."

"Yes?"

Addison bit her bottom lip. "I'm scared."

Jess smiled just a little. "You should be. You're head over heels in love. Love is about as scary as it gets. The rest . . . Well, the rest will work itself out."

∼

DETERMINED TO CLEAR HER MIND, ADDISON USED THE LADIES' room and slipped out the back door, happy to have to walk a little farther than necessary back to her car. Thankfully, the heavy rain had let up and was once again just a light drizzle. Addison glanced at her phone. Maybe she should call Patrick and ask him to dinner. She needed to tell him she was going back to work, and knowing it wasn't going to go over very well, she figured it might as well happen in a public place.

As she reached to dial her phone, it rang, startling her. "Uh. Hello."

The deep voice that responded threw her off. "You're looking incredibly beautiful today, Mrs. Greyer. That shade of blue when damp . . . Wow. Well, I have to say, it really compliments your eyes."

Addison inhaled sharply, instantly noting her surroundings. She didn't even have to ask who it was. This was one voice she'd never forget. *Stay on the phone until you get to safety. It's your best bet.*

She heard him laugh. "What? Cat got your tongue? Such a silly girl, losing your security detail like that. Don't you know I'm always watching?"

Addison picked up her pace until she was practically sprinting. *Run toward the crowd.* "You're under a restraining order, Scott. Why are you calling me?"

"Ha. Ha. Oh, you know, just a little hello for old times' sake. You get brownie points for staying away from that loser, Hartman. Such a good girl. But you fucked up, Mrs. Greyer. You know it, and I know it."

Click.

~

SONDRA LEFT THE BABY WITH THE NANNY AND SUITED UP. True to form William Hartman showed up at Sondra's place exactly to the minute, wearing faded jeans and a black T-shirt. It wasn't like William to dress so sloppily for a session. Sondra knew what this meant; he needed to be worked hard. This was William's way of asking for punishment. She knew her client well, and she understood that with everything going on he felt more out of control than ever. That was the thing about men with his persona, especially men who had been abused as children. They fed off of control, they demanded and requited it to the extreme. But they also needed an outlet in which to let it all go.

Sondra intended to give William exactly what he needed. The problem with William, though, was that every time he walked through the door, he took her breath away. She had an affinity for him that made little sense. He was the teacher's-pet type; that was for sure. Still, most of the time, he wasn't easy to like. He was demanding and hardheaded, unrelenting to his core. But it was William's charm that drew you in and held your attention. He had a gentleness you could see underneath that tough masculine exterior of his that made you want to be tougher on him and coddle him at the same time.

William entered Sondra's personal dungeon and closed the door behind him. He didn't make eye contact, but his mere presence made Sondra a little uneasy. This was nothing new. William Hartman had always been one of her favorite and most difficult clients.

He sat in the chair in the middle of the room, eyes glued to the floor. Sondra brought him the iPad and instructed him to select the music. It was all for show. It was always the same. Handing him the liquor bottle, Sondra lowered her voice. "Make me a drink. The way I like it."

William didn't meet her gaze, he never did. He was somewhere else entirely. He poured the drink with extreme care as though his life depended on it. Then he lifted the glass toward Sondra without meeting her eye. Taking a sip, she choked. "This tastes like you look. LIKE FUCKING SHIT," Sondra yelled, slamming the glass onto the floor. He was visibly startled, even though he knew what was coming. That's the thing about the power of one's mind. It's hard to shake fear that's been embedded so deeply. "You never can get it right. Can you? No," she said. " I should have expected this. That's just what happens with fuckups."

Sondra leaned over, her lips grazing William's ear as he continued to stare at the floor. "Get on your knees and pick up this goddamned mess you've made."

He didn't budge. So she took him by the hair and shoved him to the floor. Then she pressed her heel into the glass, smashing it further. Meticulously picking up every single tiny piece, William quickly found his large hands full of glass shards. He held them up toward Sondra like an offering, but she raised her nine-inch heel and drop kicked his hands, causing glass to go flying. William flinched but stayed put, eyes glued to the floor.

Sondra grabbed him by his left ear, dragging him toward the chair. "Guess you can't fucking hear either, huh? Such a worthless piece of shit, you are. A real fucking waste of space."

Placing a few glass shards on the seat of the chair, she ordered William to sit and placed a rope around his chest, tying it as tightly as she could manage. Once he was secured and bound so tightly she knew it made it difficult to breathe, she placed the blindfold. For what came next, Sondra left out the gag on purpose. William Hartman needed to be able to speak. Getting this out was imperative to his recovery; it was time to cut to the core.

"Today we're going to play a little game otherwise known as a Q&A session, okay? Can your inferior, stupid little mind grasp this concept, William?"

Head hung, William nodded.

"Good. Now what would put the idea in that small little mind of yours to have me blackmail that silly girl to come back to the company? Do you really think she wants you, William? Do you think you're capable of being loved?"

When William didn't respond, Sondra struck him across the chest with the whip. "Let's try this again. Shall we?"

It took five more lashings for William to respond. He drew in a deep breath and whispered, "Because I love her, and deep down, I know she loves me, too."

Sondra hit him again. "She left you, can't you see that? You are unlovable, aren't you?" She walked around him once and then stopped. "That's why she doesn't want to be with you. Isn't it?"

No response. *Whack.* Sondra put all of her force into it this time. William flinched as she moved closer. Weaving her fingers through his jet-black hair, she pulled hard. Her clients were always sensitive about their hair. Those that had hair, anyway. But not William. Because in his mind, he wasn't a man sitting before her, he was a boy. William reverted. Some of her clients did and some didn't. William was the worst. Sondra drew her hand back. "Answer me, William. You've got one, two—"

"Okay. OKAY! No," he said. "I mean, yes. She called it off, but she does love me. I know she does."

Sondra pulled harder. "And how do you know this, Mr. Hartman? Do you think you're capable of being loved?"

"I don't know. But with her, I believe there's the possibility."

She released his hair. "So, what you're saying is... you believe this girl loves you? That you are capable of loving and being loved?"

"Yes."

Sondra slowly untied him and removed the blindfold. She watched as he came back into himself, so to speak. It was hypnotism, for him. Always had been.

"My work here is done for today."

William shifted, winced and then smiled. "That's it?"

Sondra poured a drink and raised her glass. "Here's to the possibility, Mr. Hartman. Now get out."

William stood to go.

"Oh, and William?"

He turned and eyed her quizzically.

"If you ever fucking smile at me again in my dungeon, I'm going to make you wish you hadn't."

CHAPTER FOUR

Addison asked Patrick to meet her at their favorite downtown restaurant. The lighting was soft, and the food amazing, but the best part was the ambiance was neither too loud nor too quiet. She knew she would have her work cut out for her with her husband, but she was done with words left unspoken, with pretending everything was okay. It clearly wasn't. Even though she'd ended things with William, she'd realized that her marriage had been over a long time ago. It was time she got her life together.

Addison felt well prepared to do what she needed to do right up until the second she saw Patrick walk in. He was dressed in his business suit, tie unfastened, and Addison watched as he talked with the maître d', certain she could almost see the young man in him that she'd met on that college campus years ago. Way back when love was enough and neither of them could foresee any of the issues that would eventually lead to their demise. The only thing worse than losing her gumption in that moment, was the fact that she couldn't pinpoint just when the demise of their marriage had begun. All she knew now was that they'd each equally contributed.

Patrick spotted her and smiled. She watched him as he walked to the table, confident, and completely unaware of what he was walking into. That was Patrick, in a nutshell. He bent down to kiss her on the cheek and then quickly slid into his seat. He eyed her expectantly and then motioned to their surroundings as if to say, "What's up?"

Addison inhaled sharply as the waitress finished taking their drink order. She knew this would be difficult, she just hadn't realized *how* difficult. She'd originally chosen a glass of the house wine, but Patrick had insisted on ordering their finest champagne. He always had known how to deter her. "So—" she began.

"We've always loved this place."

"Patrick, stop—" she told him, holding up her hands. "I need to talk to you, and I need you to listen. And I mean *really* listen."

Leaning back in his chair and intertwining his hands behind his head, he smirked. "I'm all ears."

She waited, picked up her glass of water and sipped it. "I'm going back to the agency on Monday, resuming my position as an account manager," she said calmly. "I've decided that not only is it time but that it's in everyone's best interest."

"The hell it is."

Addison sighed. "Look," she started, pausing to brush her hair away from her face. "I've made my decision, and I'm letting you know. How long do you intend to keep this up, Patrick? This isn't working."

"What isn't working?" he asked. He was going to make her spell it out.

"Our marriage has been over for a long time."

"Says who?"

"I say."

"Well, I beg to differ," he countered. She watched as he folded his hands and then cracked his knuckles. "I want you to tell me you don't love me anymore, Addison. In fact, I dare you to say it," he added, leaning forward to rest his elbows on the table. "Thing is you can't, and we both know it."

So, he was going in for the kill. "Of course I do. You're the father of my children, but that isn't enough."

Patrick lowered his voice almost to a whisper. "Who says *you* get to decide what's enough?"

She shifted. "I'm not happy, Patrick. Are you?"

"I'm happy enough," he told her throwing up his hands. "Jesus, Addison, what do you want from me?"

"I want a divorce, Patrick."

He ran his fingers through his hair. "Well, there's one I've never heard before."

Addison leaned forward and looked him straight in the eye. "I'm serious, and I'm hoping that we can work together civilly so this goes as smoothly as possible for the kids."

Patrick swallowed hard. "That's bullshit, Addison. You want this to work as smoothly as possible for YOU. You don't give a fuck about them. You don't care about anyone but yourself."

She shifted uncomfortably in her chair. "That's not true. Deep down you know that, Patrick. I'm sorry you're angry. I'm sorry you find it necessary to try to blackmail me by threatening to take the boys. But I mean . . . come on. Is this really how you want it to end?"

"That's the thing," he replied. "It doesn't need to end."

"Seriously," Addison scoffed. "Have you heard nothing I've said? Does this have to be an all-out showdown? Or can we, please, just settle this like responsible adults? Like responsible parents? Please, Patrick? I want out and I'm asking you not to tie my hands here."

"Now that's an expression you know well, isn't it? You're used to being the one to tie hands. It isn't quite so fun when the tables are turned, is it?"

She sighed. "Patrick, please."

Patrick stood and walked to her side of the table. Leaning so close she could feel the heat of his breath on her ear, he whispered. "I'm not breaking my family apart unless you've got a better goddamned reason than you not being happy. Give me a fucking break, Addison. You want a divorce, huh? Well, go for it. Just don't expect me to make it easy on you as you tear our family to shreds. I know what you're up to. And good luck, sweetheart... I say, 'May the best man win.'"

And with that he turned and walked out on her.

~

PATRICK WOULD BE DAMNED IF HE'D LET HIS WIFE MAKE A FOOL out of him anymore than she already had. His life was slowly unraveling, and he had to do something about it. Okay, sure, he loved Addison, but *what* woman was worth any of this trouble? He'd always been a good husband, a little absent, maybe, but he'd always provided for his family.

He knew Addison though, and he knew that when she wanted something she'd find a way to get it. So, Patrick did what he'd always done when he was scared of losing and dialed his mother, who insisted on scheduling an appointment with the family's attorney, which was how Patrick found himself sitting in a plush office chair, staring at his wedding ring and wondering how it had come to this.

"So, let me get this right, Mrs. Greyer. Your daughter-in-law was unfaithful, is currently about to take the stand in a case where the defendant is proposing that she was involved in some sort of sex game gone bad, and you are telling me that she is planning on filing for divorce and asking for full custody of the children?"

Penny pursed her lips. "That's exactly what I'm saying."

"Patrick, how about you? Would you agree with your mother's account of the situation?"

Patrick stared blankly but said nothing.

"Patrick! For goodness' sake, answer the man," Penny chided.

The attorney cocked his head. "Is this or isn't it factual, Mr. Greyer?"

Patrick's lips formed a hard line. "It is."

"And do you also wish for a divorce?" The bald overweight man probed further. Patrick didn't care much for him, never had. He was always the first to come and the last to go at his parent's dinner parties. Always the one who laughed too loud, and drank too much. But it served its purpose. He was successful for a reason.

"No," Patrick fumed.

Penny sighed. "Oh, come on, Patrick! What is wrong with you? Just let her go already. She's been nothing but selfish. And frankly, well, you know this, I'm not sure why you married her in the first place."

The attorney cleared his throat. "Is it your intention to stall the divorce or fight for custody?"

Patrick's eyes narrowed. "Both, I guess."

Penny stood, pacing the room. "Patrick, dear, please, won't you let us talk some sense into you?"

"You know, Mrs. Greyer, your son is actually coming at this from a very good angle. By positioning himself as the scorned husband vying to keep his family together, he may actually stand a chance at getting custody. I assume the infidelity is something we can prove in court?"

Penny smiled, and Patrick stared out the window. "Absolutely," Penny said. "But I just want to reiterate that we ensure that she is to end up with nothing in the divorce. And, I do mean *nothing*. Have we made ourselves clear on that?"

"You certainly have, Mother," Patrick interjected. He stood and started toward the door before stopping to address his attorney. "I've had enough for today. You know how to reach me, should you have any further questions."

~

PENNY GREYER WAS FURIOUS WITH HER SON. FIRST, HE practically wasted the family attorney's time, but what did he care? He wasn't paying for it. This was just like Patrick, too, always leaving her to clean up the messes he'd created. Just like his father.

Secondly, not only hadn't she a clue why he'd married this woman in the first place but now she had no idea why he couldn't let go when he had a clear shot at getting out unscathed. What did this woman have over her son, besides his children? Only another mother could understand how much she abhorred this woman for ruining her son. From the moment Patrick brought her home that first time, Penny was certain Addison had been determined to undo their family. She'd made Penny out to be the bad guy; she'd made her look like the crazy one. All for what? For trying to protect her son, that's what. Yes, she'd given her the most beautiful, talented grandchildren ever, but Patrick never should've married her in the first place. Had he listened to her in the beginning, there wouldn't be this mess here for her to worry herself over. Nor would she have to have taken the drastic measures she'd undertaken. But anyone who knew Penny knew that she'd do anything if it meant keeping up appearances.

~

ADDISON SELECTED HER BEST OUTFIT, A DARK GREY FITTED dress and black pumps to wear on her first day back to the office. In many ways, the dress matched her mood. Sure, it looked nice to the casual observer, but look any deeper and you'd see the truth. The stress of the trial and life in general had caused her to lose weight, and she was constantly on edge, more so after receiving the phone call from Scott Hammons. She'd reported it to the detective handling her case, but so far, the phone number hadn't been traceable, and from the logs, it hadn't appeared that he'd broken any house arrest orders. *How then had he seen her in order to know her whereabouts?* Addison wasn't buying it and was determined to devise a plan to catch him in the act before he had the chance to do her any further harm.

As was usual on Monday morning, she met Jess at the coffee shop. This morning, she had arrived a few minutes early and sat sipping her coffee, trying to settle herself until a familiar voice interrupted. "Good morning, Mrs. Greyer."

Addison looked up to see none other than William Hartman standing before her. The mere sight of him rendered her speechless, unable to formulate a coherent sentence.

"Well then, I guess it's nice to see you, too," he said. William eyed the empty chair.

"May I sit?"

She glanced over at the seat, still unsure what to say. William took the seat, propping one knee on the other. "It's okay," he told her. "I don't mind conversing with myself. You see the thing is, I got your letter," he added, twisting his lips. "And to tell you the truth, I didn't much care for it."

Addison frowned and traced her finger around the lid of her coffee cup. *So, he's going to play it this way. Nice.* She looked up. "I wasn't aware I had asked your opinion on the matter."

William threw his head back and let out a deep-throated laugh. "Ah. See. Therein lies the problem. You really should have."

She cocked her head and studied his face. *God, how she wanted to reach out and touch him.* "What happened to your face?"

"What's wrong with my face?" he asked, running his fingers along his jaw.

"The bruise."

"Nothing. We're not talking about bruises here, Addison."

"Aren't we though?"

"Hey, sweetie, sorry I'm late," Jess interrupted, placing her coffee cup on the table between them.

William and Addison both stood, but neither of them took their eyes off the other. "Jess, this is William Hartman. William, this is, Jessica."

William turned slowly toward Jess and extended his hand. "It's a pleasure to meet you, Jessica," he said. Then he turned his attention back to Addison. "Well, I really should be running, so we'll finish this up later? Word has it you'll be in the office today."

Addison raised her brow but words wouldn't come. She bit her lip. *Fuck,* she thought sinking back in her chair. She watched as William strode confidently out the door.

Jess cleared her throat, clearly enthralled with what had just taken place. "Yeah, okay, so I get it. That man is . . . Well, he's... Whatever—" she said, sighing. "You know what I mean."

Addison pinched the bridge of her nose. "Incredulous, is the word I think you're looking for."

"Right," Jess said. "But what in bloody hell was that all about? So much for ending it, huh?"

Addison rolled her eyes. "Yeah, I guess."

"Girl, you are so in over your head," Jess said, studying her face. "You do know that, right?"

Addison chewed at her bottom lip, shook her head, and then changed the subject to the only thing that made sense to say. "I asked Patrick for a divorce, Jess. My attorney is filing Wednesday."

Jessica drew in a deep breath and held it. "He's not going to let go easily, is he?"

"No, he's not," she replied, feeling her throat tighten.

Jess nodded. "Hey-—on the bright side—you're not even sure which of them I'm talking about, are you?"

Addison shot her a look that could kill. "Ha. I'm afraid there isn't a bright side in this situation."

The two of them sat in silence for a long while before Jess spoke again. "I want you to know that I'm here for you, Addison, no matter what. Always know that I'm in your corner."

"I know," Addison told her. "It helps, believe me."

"Oh, and you know there's always a silver lining, right?"

Addison shrugged.

"Well, there is. Sometimes you just have to look really hard to find it."

Addison finished off her coffee and smiled weakly. "Can I get that embroidered on a pillow or something?"

Jess winked at her. "I think that can be arranged."

～

ADDISON WALKED THE FEW BLOCKS TO HER OFFICE, FEELING uneasy, certain that she was being watched. It was only a matter of time before Scott Hammons would strike again, and Addison knew she had to be preemptive.

Walking into the office, she noticed not much had changed, except the receptionist at the front desk, that is.

"I'm Ruby," the girl's peppy voice exclaimed. "You must be Addison."

She extended her hand. "Hi, Ruby."

The peppy brunette handed over a stack of papers. "Here's your itinerary for the day. Ms. Sheehan said she will see you as soon as you get settled in," she told Addison breathlessly, before pausing. "Oh, and this was left for you."

Addison eyed the stationery. *Hmm.* "Thank you, Ruby. Please let Sondra know that I'll be ready for her in my office in ten minutes." *It's best to play on home field if given the chance.*

Closing her office door, she grabbed the letter opener and carefully sliced through the envelope. Addison impatiently pulled out the note, knowing exactly who'd sent it.

Dearest Addison,

You are wrong about many things, but I'll start with this: I did want to hear from you, that day, today, and every day in between. I love you, Addison, and I know you love me, too. But love isn't always that simple; this I understand.

The thing is, I've spent a great deal of my life loving people who never loved me in return. I can see that you have, too, and I think perhaps that's just a small part of why I fell in love with you. Despite what you tell me, underneath it all, I believe that there's a girl who, just like me, wants to love and be loved—she just can't quite figure out how to go about it. Well, I want that girl to know that the story doesn't end here. She'll figure it out. My greatest hope is that we'll figure it out together. I'd like that girl to know that all she has to do is to take my hand and jump. I'll be her soft landing.

I realize that you need me to let go right now, just as you have asked. And so, I will.

But I'll end with this: I believe I've loved you before, Addison, in another time, in another place. And I will love you again. Just wait and see.

All my love,
William

CHAPTER FIVE

Sondra was in her element, throwing orders left and right. Addison hadn't caught any of them until Sondra slapped her hand on the desk, knocking her out of her reverie. "Damn it, Addison," she seethed. "What in the hell is it now?"

Addison shifted in her chair and sat up straighter. "I'm sorry."

Sondra gazed at her. "Well?" she asked, widening her eyes. "Let's have it."

She exhaled. "I'm filing for a divorce. Scott Hammons is watching me. I guess you could say things are a little rough right now…"

Her boss did a double take. "Good grief… Have you contacted the police?"

She nodded. "Yeah, but they weren't much help."

Sondra crossed the room and took a seat in front of Addison. "I assume Mr. Hartman's staff is still protecting you."

"Something like that."

"Well, we're going to have to do something about this, aren't we?"

"I'm working on it."

Sondra furrowed her brow. "I see. And the divorce? Why now?"

"Why *not* now?" Addison quipped.

"I don't know," Sondra told her. "It just seems that you have a lot going on; that's all. Did you really need to add to it?"

Addison's gaze drifted toward the floor-to-ceiling windows. "I'm moving out this weekend. I've rented a little place not far from our house and I've hired movers. Patrick has no idea, of course, and I haven't told the boys. I just have to get out."

"Jesus," Sondra said, closing her eyes.

"I know. It's a lot," she replied, looking back at Sondra. "But I'm suffocating. If I tell him I'm leaving, he'll make it impossible for me to go. I didn't want it to end this way..."

Sondra inhaled sharply. "We never do," she said, with a sigh. Then she raised her voice, making it sound more cheery than she was. Sondra was not a cheery person and she wasn't at all good at faking it. "Do you need anything? I assume you're satisfied with your new salary."

"No," Addison said. "I mean, yes. I'm good."

"Good," Sondra smiled.

Addison cleared her throat. "You know part of me always knew that it would end up this way, that he'd never let me go easily. That's why I said yes to your offer. Most people have trouble understanding that, but I guess they'd have to know Patrick to really get it. He's never failed at anything in his life because he's avoided failure at all costs. Our marriage is no different. That's what he does; if he doesn't like the rules, he refuses to even play the game. At some point along the way, he just stopped participating. I knew that deep down he wasn't all he seemed to be, and so I saved. I saved for attorneys' fees. I saved for a place of our own. I put a lot of my salary aside so the boys and I would never have to be dependent on his participation again. That's why I did what I did, saying yes to working at Seven. I did it for the money, sure, but also for the person I became. Working at Seven changed me. It showed me what freedom could be like. And it gave me the independence to make it happen."

Sondra grasped the door handle and turned to face Addison. "My work as a Dominatrix has been the best part of my life."

Addison pressed her lips together. She knew that was Sondra's way of saying she understood.

Sondra turned the door handle and then glanced back at Addison. "I'll have everything I just went over typed up and emailed to you within the hour."

She nodded.

"Oh—and Addison?"

She raised her brow quizzically.

"I'm betting on this not affecting your work here."

"It won't. You have my word," Addison promised.

Sondra opened the door slightly and then closed it again. "Addison, it behooves me not to get involved in such matters. For what it's worth though, I think you're doing the right thing," she told her with a long sigh. "Your timing just sucks, that's all."

~

Dear William,

I'm writing because I want you to hear this from me and me alone. I've filed for divorce. While this doesn't change anything between us or where things stand, I do want to thank you. Had we not met, I never would've had the courage to end my marriage.

It's unfortunate for all involved that things worked out the way they did. Let's just agree that our love was chronologically challenged from the beginning. :)

Your letter was beautiful. I thank you for that, too. And you're right. I do love you. But the truth of the matter is I need to love myself before I can really love anyone else.

I'm working on that.

Take care,
Addison

ADDISON SEALED THE ENVELOPE, DIALED HER CONTACT, AND then the courier. Once the letter had been picked up, she gathered her things and rushed over to her attorney's office.

The office, located just around the corner from the Hartman building, was large and sterile. *Maybe attorneys' offices weren't meant to be inviting place*s, Addison thought as she rounded the corner. Her breath caught, and a lump formed in her throat as she took in the sight of paparazzi gathered just outside her attorney's office. *Keep calm,* she reminded herself. Maybe they're here for someone else, she considered, although logic pointed to the contrary. As she entered the doors, she focused her eyes straight ahead and did her best to ignore the flurry of questions being shouted and the cameras that were shoved in her direction.

Once inside the building, Addison decided to take the stairs in an attempt to buy time and compose herself. *Someone had obviously tipped the press off, and this wasn't good.* Taking a deep breath, she opened the heavy glass doors and made her way in. Addison searched the lobby for a receptionist, and when she didn't see one seated at the desk, she simply took a seat in the waiting room and waited. Her attorney, Thomas Bradbury, was a shark known for winning at all costs. He wasn't friendly and he wasn't charming. He was closed off, and also, a client at Seven. She knew she shouldn't mix the two, but she also knew she needed someone she could trust. And, more importantly, someone who could win. Addison reached for a magazine as a petite older woman opened the door, nodded in her direction, and asked her to follow. After being led down a series of halls, Addison was ushered into a large conference room. At the end of the table sat the man she'd hired to handle her divorce.

Tom Bradbury looked like an oversized jock clad in an expensive looking three-piece suit and was positioned confidently with his legs propped on the table as he impatiently barked orders into his phone. Next to him sat a younger looking version of himself, who appeared to be furiously jotting down notes. "Good. Then it's a done deal. I assume you'll have the proposed settlement sent over by COB," he ordered.

Slamming the phone down, he stood and grinned brilliantly at the young man sitting next to him. "And that's how it's done."

He turned and eyed Addison up and down in a way that only a man of his kind would. "You must be Addison Greyer. Wow. Tom Bradbury," he said, playing coy. It was important on both sides to be discreet about any ties to Seven. It was a rule, in fact. He smiled. "But I'm sure you knew that already," he added, thrusting his hand in her direction. Addison narrowed her eyes as he continued. "What a pleasure. A real pleasure, I must say. You're even more beautiful in person than the image I've seen floating around in the media," he laughed. "You never know with those things."

So, he lives up to his reputation. Addison shifted her attention to the man standing next to Bradbury. "Oh," he said. "And this here is my associate, Liam Mott. He'll be observing and helping with your case."

Addison extended her hand, suddenly noting how boyish Liam Mott looked. There was something warm in the way he smiled at her, and Addison surmised that he must be fresh out of law school. *Just a kid.*

After smoothing her dress, she sat down and eyed the men expectantly but didn't speak.

Both attorneys followed suit. "Well, okay, then. Let's get started, shall we?" Tom commanded. "I assume that you've completed the tasks we discussed over the phone."

Addison cleared her throat. He was testing her outside of Seven. She should just let it be. But she couldn't. It was time to put him in his place. This was the sort of thing that had to be done with the Tom Bradbury's of the world. Never give 'em an inch. It just turns out bad that way. "Mr. Bradbury," Addison said, looking at his associate. "You've come highly recommended, and I appreciate your taking me on as a client. But one thing you should never do is assume anything about me." She turned toward Tom again. "If we're going to work together, I'm going to need confirmation of that."

Tom smiled, and then an expression Addison knew well crossed his face. "Of course," he said. "Perhaps we've gotten off on the wrong foot. Let's start over, shall we?" Whether he was willing to admit it or not, Tom Bradbury wanted confirmation that Addison was who she said she was, both in and out of the dungeon. He *needed* that. And she was willing to give it to him. *Always play the part.*

"As far as the tasks you suggested, no. I went a different

route. I've rented a place a few blocks from home and hired movers to come this Saturday."

Tom Bradbury pursed his lips. "Um... why? That wasn't what we discussed at all. Have you changed the bank accounts? What about withdrawing half of the contents?" he asked cocking his head. "Have you taken care of that?"

Addison shifted and straightened in the chair. "No."

The attorneys glanced at one another before Mr. Bradbury cleared his throat and spoke slowly. "May I ask why not?"

"I don't want any of the money. He earned it. He should keep it. Look— I know Patrick isn't going to move out willingly— so that leaves me no choice but to go myself. Do I want to remove my children from the only home they've ever known? No. I just don't see any other option."

"Huh," he said, pursing his lips. "I can't advise you any of those things are the best plan of action."

Addison shrugged.

"Let me ask you this, Mrs. Greyer. Has your husband ever been abusive? I want you to think about it really hard, now. A little shove here or there? You know how it goes with married folks, it happens."

She didn't miss a beat. "No."

"How about being verbally or emotionally abusive? Has he ever called you names?"

Addison sighed, long and slow. "Other than trying to keep me in a marriage I no longer want to be in, no."

Tom Bradbury stood abruptly and walked over to a mini bar in the corner of the room. "May I pour you a drink, Mrs. Greyer?"

"No. Thank you."

"Well, I hope you won't mind if I have one myself," he stated as Addison watched him toss the amber liquid back. "Here's the deal," the attorney continued. "I'm going to be blatantly honest with you. If you refuse to follow the advice I give you, I don't think you stand a chance of getting anything in this divorce, maybe not *even* your children. For one, you've admitted to being unfaithful. Hell, it's been splashed all over the media. You're currently about to take the stand in a trial which suggests that you're into some— what are they calling it? Oh, yeah, some sort of sick deviant behavior at best and prostitution at worst. So, I have to say, it's not looking very good for you, Mrs. Greyer."

"I'm not paying you to tell me how it looks."

Tom Bradbury chuckled, but only slightly. "Well then, tell me. What exactly is it you are paying me for?"

"Well, I hear you're the best. The thing is, I don't want to drag Patrick through the mud. I don't want our divorce to turn into a spectacle, tit for tat. I'm hoping to keep this simple, especially for our children. I don't want anything from him. He can have it all. I'm perfectly capable of supporting our children on my own if he doesn't want to. And I'm not expecting anything from him. I just want out. He can have visitation on his terms, but I want full custody. Particularly given his work has him out of the country on a regular basis. He's been unfaithful too, and while I don't want to, I'm prepared to bring that up if it comes down to it. Oh, and I haven't engaged in any form of prostitution EVER. So—let's get that straight."

"Well, this just gets better and better. But you aren't going to win that way, if that's what you're after and I assume with so much at stake, it is," Bradbury exclaimed, pouring himself another drink.

Addison pushed her chair back, away from the massive desk and eyed Tom. "Do you have children, Mr. Bradbury?"

The attorney hesitated. "I do."

"Then I'm sure you can imagine wanting to do anything you could to protect them, while at the same time wanting to keep their innocence for just a little longer. They're my first priority here. I'm prepared to fight, but only if I need to. So, I guess my question is this: are you willing to play by my rules? Because if not . . . I'm fine with taking a referral and calling it a day."

"If it's all right, I have an idea," the young man interrupted.

Addison and Bradbury's eyes darted toward Liam.

"Oh Jesus, let's hear it," Tom replied, rubbing his temples.

"What if we just feel them out? What if we file the paperwork and see what happens? Perhaps, they'll just agree to our demands."

Addison smiled. *She liked this kid.* Tom exhaled loudly. "That is the worst fucking idea I've ever heard. For starters, any attorney worth his salt knows you want to be on the offensive."

The kid continued, "Mrs. Greyer, what is the one thing you know your husband doesn't want out there? Based on the research I've done, I know that affairs between colleagues, especially between higher ups and their subordinates, are forbidden within the company he works for. Isn't it correct that he received a promotion that led to his leaving the family for the better part of last year?"

She really liked this kid. "Yes, it is."

"And would it be correct to assume that this affair between your husband and his boss began before *this* promotion?"

She exhaled. "If I had to guess, I'd say it did."

"Huh. Actually, you know... I think I like where this is going," Tom Bradbury interjected.

The kid stood. "My idea is to file and let Mr. Greyer's attorneys know up front that we intend to call the mistress in—if we have to go to trial, that is," he said. He glared at Tom Bradbury. "I always find it interesting what people will agree to when a little pressure is applied in the right spot."

Bradbury slapped the kid on the back. "I knew I hired you for a reason. That was exactly the approach I was gonna suggest, seeing that Mrs. Greyer kicked my legs out from under me, anyway. Usually, I'm all for playing hardball, but I really think we're onto something here. This could definitely be a good angle," he said turning to Addison. "Mrs. Greyer, what do you say?"

"Patrick lives for his work. It's the one thing he'd hate to lose more than his 'ideal family.' But I want it clear to all involved that I don't want anything from him aside from a divorce and custody of our children."

Bradbury's phone buzzed. He picked it up and stared at the screen as he nodded. "That's very noble, Addison. Just not very smart."

She raised her brow. "What can I say?"

Tom shook his head. "All right, we'll have the papers drawn up and sent over for you to sign tomorrow morning."

Addison stood, extended her hand to Liam, and thanked him.

She walked toward the door then turned on her heel, eyeing Tom Bradbury, who was still lost in his phone. "Tom, I appreciate you agreeing to go about it this way. I know you think I'm being foolish. You see, the thing is, I know my husband. And I know what he responds to or rather what he *doesn't* respond to, for that matter. Just to be clear, I'm prepared to play dirty. I just hope it doesn't come to that."

Tom looked up and met Addison's gaze, his expression grim. "Let's hope for your sake, it doesn't."

~

PENNY GREYER SHOWED UP WITH CASH, A DISPOSABLE PHONE,

details as to Addison's whereabouts, and a shared goal to mentally drive her to the brink. She was going to make harassing that little gold-digger easy. Little did Penny know, Scott Hammons had so much more in store.

He'd already decided he was going after her instead of that varmint Hartman, who had not only taken the business that HE'D built but who had driven his family away and sucked the life right out of him. William Hartman should've been smart enough to know that if you play with fire you get burned. Mess with the wrong person and eventually it will catch up with you. Plus, she was easier to get to than William. And it would hurt more. *Maximum effect.*

Scott's defense team had assured him that their defense strategy was foolproof. In his favor was the fact that he had no ties to Addison. He was brilliant in that way. He'd never been in any sort of trouble before because he was too much of a genius to get caught. Seeing that there were no ties to Hartman's whore, it was going to be really hard to prove motive, further proving his brilliance. He hadn't done anything wrong but was merely a client. This defense wouldn't have been his first preference. But then it's much better to have the world think of him as someone with no morals rather than a monster.

So, yes, for the time being, he was fine with this ridiculous cat-and-mouse game Penny wanted to play with Addison Greyer. But the good news was that thanks to her dime, he'd be off of house arrest soon. Then all would be fair game. And it was high time to settle the score.

CHAPTER SIX

The last thing Patrick needed right now was for his boss and mistress to return to the States. In China, he could manage her. It was simple that way. A few phone calls here and there and several emails a day were all he had to offer to keep her at bay. Michele knew Patrick needed to stay State-side right now due to the unfortunate situation with his wife. He had explained that Addison had a long recovery ahead of her—even though that part was mostly a lie—and that he couldn't leave now. Michele had taken it better than he'd expected, which made her return visit home all the more worrisome. Things had been going as he'd planned. Now she'd urged him to take a weekend and go away with her, the way they used to do in the beginning. This was the thing about women, they always wanted everything to be the way it used to be. Only nothing ever was.

At first Patrick refused. He wouldn't let Michele get the best of him. She was good at that. Always had been. But now, things would be different. They had to be. It had been a little over a month since he'd returned home, and he was in the middle of desperately trying to save his marriage. He thought it would be an easy fix, at first. Flowers here, cards there. Being extra attentive. All the things he knew women liked. And still, it hadn't worked. He'd done everything he could think of to try and win Addison's favor, to try and change her mind. So, after two weeks of trying to seduce his own wife for Christ's sake, Patrick felt he deserved a little something for his efforts.

Since Addison wasn't giving him any, and it didn't appear that she was going to budge anytime soon, he'd decided to give into Michele. What could it hurt? "A man has needs," his father had always told him, and Patrick was no different. In any case, given the incident with the lawyer and all the talk of divorce, maybe Michele was right. Maybe a weekend away would do him some good, after all. Well, that and the fact he intended to show Addison he was secure. *Absence makes the heart grow fonder.* He would show her he was confident enough things were going to work out that he was stepping away. Perhaps, they both just needed a cooling off period, he'd said. He was right. Just as he'd predicted, it wasn't the cards or flowers that did the trick. It was his wife seeing that he was taking the lead. For the past few weeks, especially ever since they'd run into William Hartman, Addison had seemed indifferent and a little sad. That is until the morning he told her he was going away for the weekend. The moment he said it she changed into the sweet, encouraging wife he'd remembered her to be. For a moment, he almost wanted to call the whole trip off, but she seemed so happy about his "fishing trip" that he considered that maybe it was all going as planned. He'd go and see Michele and end things once and for all.

∼

PATRICK PACKED HIS BAG AS HIS WIFE SAT IN THE CHAISE
lounge, pretending to read. He knew she wasn't actually
reading because she hadn't turned a page in ages. He couldn't
quite place the look on her face.

"Earth to Addison . . ."

She looked up.

"Hey, are you sure you think this is a good idea? Me
leaving right now?"

She eyed him quizzically but said nothing.

"I mean, with Scott Hammons on the loose... I really
think maybe I should stay."

"I'll be fine," she assured him.

"Good," he said, relieved. "I'm pretty sure he won't try
anything. You know . . . The more I think about it, the more I
wonder if everything that happened between you two wasn't
just a bad misunderstanding."

She shifted, pulling her legs out from under her and
glared at him. "Wow. You're serious?"

Patrick glanced at his wife and resumed packing. "I don't
know, Addison. I guess I was just hoping we could put all of
this behind us. Sooner rather than later."

"Hm."

He raised his shoulders and dropped them. Then he
rolled his neck. "So, what do you say? Should I stay? I mean...
I haven't even gotten to say goodbye to the boys. I hate to call
from the road."

"You should go, Patrick. We're fine here," she replied
flatly.

"Yeah, I know. But hey, I was thinking... maybe when I
get back, you and I could go away together and leave the
boys with my mom like we used to in the old days."

"I don't think so, Patrick," she told him, meeting his eye.
"Nothing has changed for me. I still want a divorce."

He rolled his eyes and wheeled his luggage toward the

door before slowly turning back. He walked back to his wife, leaned down, and kissed the top of her head. "You just need time," he assured her. "I think this weekend will do us both some good. Tell the boys I love them and that I'll call them from the road, okay?"

Addison placed her book down on the chair and sat up straight. "We're moving out, Patrick."

He halted abruptly just inside the doorframe. He turned back. "Addison, come on," he said, his face growing red. "Right now isn't the time for this."

"This isn't about timing. I wanted to let you know."

Patrick shook his head, turned and started down the stairs. Halfway down, he decided he wanted to have the last word. "Take this weekend and think it over, all right? I think a little breather will do you some good."

She refused to let him have it. *That's how women are.* "I'm sure," she called out as he dug for his keys. When he turned around, she was standing just behind him. "Have a good time," she said. "We'll talk when you get back."

Patrick glanced over his shoulder at his wife. "Now, that's the girl I know and love." He turned for the door and hesitated a second before walking out, not quite realizing that life, as they knew it, was about to drastically change.

~

WILLIAM SHOWED UP FOR HIS SECOND SESSION OF THE WEEK, five minutes late. Sondra knew William; she knew this wasn't good. He stopped just inside the door of her apartment and leaned against the wall, waiting. Dressed in his usual three-piece business suit, Sondra couldn't help but notice how worn down he looked. In the past, this would've been one of those times that Sondra invited him to her bedroom following their session, but this time she wasn't so sure that even that would help. In addition, she no longer wanted to get involved with William in that way. They'd both grown beyond being each other's lover. Besides, there was too much animosity there. He'd come to her for one thing and one thing only. And Sondra knew better than to turn a powerful man like William away.

He cleared his throat, getting her attention. "I apologize for being late."

Sondra noticed the redness around his eyes and the soft lines forming across his face as he squeezed at the bridge of his nose. "Is everything all right, Mr. Hartman?"

She hated using pleasantries with someone she was so familiar with, but that was business. Respect was rule one as a Dominatrix.

"Yeah," he said. "Why are we standing around out here?" he asked, all manners aside. "Oh—and hey, look, no marks above the neck today," he added, dusting an invisible piece of lint from his jacket. "I have a business dinner following our appointment..."

Sondra frowned. "William, if it's okay with you, I'd like to try something different today. I think you're ready for it." Sondra hesitated, pointing toward her living area. "What if we start out here this evening just talking?"

William shook his head, slowly. "I'm not here for fucking therapy, Sondra. If therapy was what I wanted, that's where I'd be right now. But I'm not, I'm here."

"I can see that."

"So, let's just get to it, all right? Cut the shit, and don't hold anything back today. Except for marks above the neck, that is. I need this..."

Time for a different approach. Sondra perched herself on the edge of her sofa. "Have you heard from Addison?"

William looked surprised. "No," he said. "Why do you ask?"

57

Sondra patted the sofa. "Mr. Hartman, please, sit."

He was reluctant. But then, she'd said the magic word, and it wasn't please. "What is this about, Sondra? I haven't got time for any BS today." Still, he didn't budge.

"Have I ever bullshitted you? Now, look. You're in my home, and it's my understanding that you're here for a session. So, from this moment forward, I expect you to show some respect. Otherwise— get out."

He exhaled, that's how she knew she'd won.

Sondra narrowed her eyes. "Am I clear?"

William ran his fingers through his hair, which she noticed was a little longer than he usually kept it. All signs pointed to the fact that he was falling apart. Most of the time men like William could function well enough in the real world. Many of them were successful, powerful even. But under extreme stress and without proper care, they quickly unraveled, which was exactly what had been happening with William when he'd found Sondra and they'd begun working together.

William eyed the sofa and sat down. "You're right. I'm sorry."

"Tell me what's going on, William." Sondra asked, studying his face.

"It's just been a rough week," he sighed. "We've had issue upon issue, trying to close on a few deals."

Sondra cocked her head to the side. "Is that all? Are you having flashbacks? Have the nightmares returned?"

"Why are you asking all of this?"

"It's my job. I need to know if what we're doing in our sessions is working. Judging by the looks of you, it isn't," Sondra replied.

"Okay, then. Fine. You're right. All of it. I'm not sleeping. I can't concentrate. She's all I think about, and I just don't know what to do about any of it. I thought if I just got her back to the office that I could win her back, but it's not working. Sure, I could resort to my usual tactics, but you know what? With her, it's different. I don't want to hurt her. And that's what would happen. She asked for space, so I've given it to her. But it's fucking killing me. She's leaving him, and yet she still doesn't want me."

"What is it about her that's different, William? Why do you care so much?"

He stood and walked to the window. "Everything. She cares. She's not like me, Sondra. Hell, she's not even like you. She really, actually, cares about people. She's leaving him, but she won't let me help her," he said, balling his fists. "God, why can't she see that I just want to help? I want to make her life better."

"Would you respect her if she came running to you? Or is part of what makes her different the fact that she's never asked you for anything?"

"Yes. Maybe?" He shrugged. "I don't know."

Sondra lowered her voice. "What makes you think that people like you and I *don't* care?"

"Because we don't. We do whatever it is we need to do to get what we want. It's as simple as that. But Addison, she wants to do the right thing— or at least whatever it is she *thinks* is the right thing."

"Do you think it is? The right thing?"

William turned and stared Sondra dead in the eye. "The right thing for who?"

"For you?"

He scoffed and then shook his head. "It's complicated. That's what I think. And it's selfish of me to want her. I mean . . . Look at me. I can barely take care of myself."

"I don't think you really believe that though, do you, William?"

William squared his jaw. "No. Not really. That's the thing,

I don't even know what I really believe. Is that what you want to hear? What is it you want from me, anyway?" He threw his hands up. "What are we doing here?"

"We're talking." Sondra said. Then she stood and walked into the kitchen. She returned with a glass and a bottle of whiskey. "Make me a drink, William. Then get on your knees."

William's demeanor changed and then he did as he was told.

Sondra ran her fingers through his hair, grabbing a handful. "Do you have anything against talking, William? Tell me, why is such a simple concept so hard for you to understand?"

William glared at the floor. Finally, he shook his head.

"Now, we're going to play a little game. Do you understand? You're used to getting your way. But guess what, pretty boy? Not here— and not now. I'm going to ask the questions, and you're going to answer. Is that fair?"

Sondra tugged on his tie, cutting off his air supply. "Are we clear?"

"Yes, Mistress," William choked out.

Sondra pulled his hair tighter as she whispered in his ear. "Good. So... you love this girl. Is that correct?"

"Yes."

"And what do you think she would say if she saw you like this? Do you think she would care then?"

William grinned through the pain. "Yes."

Sondra loosened her grip on his hair and tugged his tie tighter. "That's it. Now we're getting somewhere. You see, Mr. Hartman. You're smarter than you give yourself credit for."

He inhaled deeply.

Sondra backhanded him as hard as she could.

William brought his hand to his face and wiped the blood

from his nose. "What the fuck, Sondra? I told you nothing above the neck."

"Oh, please, stop being such a pansy. For heaven's sake, do you really think the girl would be ripping apart her family if she weren't in love with you? I mean seriously, William, where are your balls? What you need to do is quit having a one-person pity party and fucking do something! Clean yourself up. Get it together."

William stood up. "I'm done here."

Sondra placed her hands on her hips and studied her client. "Hang on," she said eventually. "Let me get you an ice pack to go."

William eyed his swelling eye in the hallway mirror. "Motherfucker. I thought I made it clear I have a meeting."

Sondra tossed the icepack, and William caught it mid-air. "Let me make something clear to you. It's time to man up, William. While you've been busy licking your wounds, Scott Hammons has been harassing your girl. He's made contact with her. And if I had to guess, I'd say she hasn't told you a thing about it..."

God damn it, was all William could manage before he rushed out the door.

There wasn't a doubt in Sondra's mind where he was headed. This may have been her best work yet. Finally, now, they were getting somewhere.

~

WILLIAM CAUGHT CARL OFF GUARD WHEN HE GRABBED HIM BY the collar just outside Sondra's doorway. "Are our guys still detailing Mrs. Greyer?"

Carl swiftly grabbed William's wrists and maneuvered himself away. "Mr. Hartman, I kindly ask that you keep your hands off me, or this will be the end of our working relationship."

William backed away, gritting his teeth. "I'm sorry, Carl. But, please, just answer the question."

"Yes, sir, we have three guys on her," he replied, stepping away. He straightened his collar.

William started for the stairs. "Take me to her."

"Sir, please, calm down," Carl replied. Then hurriedly whispered orders into his earpiece.

"I'm not going to fucking calm down. Don't *tell* me to calm down. That bastard contacted her, and what I want to know is why in the hell I haven't heard about it."

Carl opened the car door, ushered William in and ordered the driver and the man seated in the passenger side to drive to Addison's.

"Don't worry," he promised. "I'm going to get to the bottom of this."

William rubbed his swollen eye and winced. "Damn straight you are. And from now on, you're the point man on her security detail. I'm not taking any more chances."

~

JESSICA HAD KINDLY OFFERED TO TAKE THE BOYS FOR THE night so that Addison could begin packing the stuff she didn't want the movers to touch. She wasn't taking much, so as not to upset Patrick, and she'd already picked out and purchased much of the furniture and belongings for the new house with assistance from some of the employees at the agency. Thankfully, Sondra had been extremely helpful, throwing assistance her way that she hadn't even realized she'd need.

In the morning, Addison would pick the boys up and tell them about the move. She was dreading it. They'd been so excited to sleep over at Aunt Jessica's, and she felt terrible, thinking about all of the changes they would all face over the next several months. Addison had just placed the last of her favorite coffee mugs into the box when her cell phone chimed. She read and then reread the text message.

Mrs. Greyer, I'm coming in through the side entrance. We need to talk.

It was from Richard, the man in charge of her security detail. With everything going on, the message unsettled her even further. While she didn't really enjoy being followed or having to announce her every whim, she had grown fond of the men, baking them cookies that she'd allowed the boys to deliver, along with the custom artwork they'd made for them.

Addison heard the key turn in the lock at the back door. She poured herself a glass of wine. "In here," she called over her shoulder, before bringing the glass to her lips. Addison looked up and then blinked, attempting to swallow the lump that had just lodged in her throat. She did a double take before her brain could process what she was seeing. *Yes, it really was him standing in front of her.*

William stood there staring for a moment before he finally spoke. "Why didn't you tell me about Hammons contacting you?"

She gulped down the wine in her glass, and when she found it empty, she poured another. "Would you like a drink?"

William lowered his gaze. "No. I'd *like* you to answer my question."

"What are you doing here?" Addison surveyed her kitchen. "You know we're not supposed to have any contact with one another. My attorneys tell me it's the worst thing I could do for myself."

"I don't care what your attorneys think. I asked you a question," William said, moving closer.

Addison backed away ever so slightly. "Oh— I don't know — probably because I expected you to do something like this."

William moved in for the kill, his eyes on hers. He grabbed her by the waist and pushed her against the counter. He held her in place with his body. They stood staring at one another, searching the other's eyes for words, or for answers, that wouldn't seem to come. Finally, William pulled her in tight. He buried his face in her hair and inhaled. "Damn it, Addison," he whispered. "I'm not sure whether to make love to you or kill you."

"That's always a good combination."

He pulled back. "This isn't a joke. Do you know how fucking scared I was when I heard that asshole is bothering you again? I was sure he'd hurt you, and I had to see for myself."

Addison furrowed her brow. "Well, as you can see, I'm fine."

"Why are you here alone? And God damn it, Addison, why didn't I know about him contacting you? Why didn't my security know about it?"

Addison shrugged. Maybe it was the wine, or maybe it was him, but she felt faint. She pushed away, putting some distance between them, for the first time seeing William's face up close. She gasped. "What in the hell happened to your face?"

William reached for his eye instinctively. "Nothing."

"Hold on," she said, stepping back further to get a better look. Addison inhaled and held it. "I'm going to ask you again. What happened to your face, William?"

He shook his head. "It's nothing."

Addison reached for the wine bottle and poured herself another glass. "So, you're seeing Sondra again, huh?"

William chuckled and then took the glass from her hand. "Maybe it was Hammons. Why do you care anyway?"

Addison reached for her glass, but William was much too strong to wrestle it away from. "Oh, I don't know, probably for the same reason you're here. Wait. *Why* are you here, again?"

She's pissed. Hmmm. That's a good sign. William took her by her wrist and flipped her around so that her back was to his stomach. *Her mouth might be telling him she was pissed, but her body certainly wasn't.* "Because I need you, Addison. Because I'm a mess without you. But most of all because I love you, and I'm tired of hiding it."

She couldn't speak. It was just too much, having him this close. She could feel every inch of his body on hers. Skin on skin, clothing on clothing, it didn't matter. She could feel the heat of his breath on her neck, and she was quickly losing the will to fight. "William, please."

William traced her ear with his tongue. "I've always liked it best when you beg, you know."

She blew all the air out of her lungs.

"Just stop fighting it, Addison. Stop fighting us," he sighed. "Can't you see you aren't going to win?"

"It's not about winning."

"Fine. Let me make love to you, and the rest, we'll sort out later."

Spoken like a man. Addison used one of the self-defense moves she'd learned to untangle herself and swiftly jabbed William in the ribs.

"You seriously think I'm that easy, do you?"

William groaned and tried to pull himself upright. "It worked the first time, didn't it?"

Addison deadpanned. "Fuck you, William," she seethed. "That was a low blow."

"Tell me about it," he grinned.

Addison shook her head, downed the last of her wine, and surveyed the mess around her. "You wanna get out of here?"

William reached for her hand and interlaced his fingers with hers. "I've never wanted anything more."

CHAPTER SEVEN

Addison climbed into the dark SUV with William close behind. She whispered the directions to Carl who simply nodded.

William looked at Addison in disbelief. "Where are you taking me?"

She gave him a sideways glance, and then a sly smile before scooting over in the seat, putting some distance between the two of them. "You'll see."

"Whatever you say," William replied, closing the distance. "I've missed you," he added and Addison could feel his gaze in her periphery. "God, you have no idea how much I've missed you."

Addison again shifted over, needing space to breathe, room to think. *What was it about this man that made her lose all rationality?* "There's a lot we need to talk about, William."

William pressed the button to put up the privacy divider between the two of them and the men upfront. He glared at her. "So talk."

"We will," she said, staring out the window. "There's a time and place for everything."

~

ADDISON AND WILLIAM PULLED UP TO THE UNASSUMING building they'd both come to know as Seven. William cocked an eyebrow. She glanced over at him. "Really? You want to talk here?"

She shrugged. "We're here, aren't we?"

Once inside, Addison ordered William into room number two. He was to wait for her, just the same as always, by sitting in the chair in the center of the room. She needed to get changed. He knew the routine. *They both knew the routine.*

She entered the room, dressed in the leather catsuit she'd worn before, only this time without the mask. William eyed her from head to toe, seemingly amused. She walked to where he sat, bent down, and pecked him on the cheek. Then she asked him to press play on her phone. He seemed surprised when Radiohead's "Fake Plastic Trees" belted out instead of the usual.

Addison lifted one of the riding crops from the table, carefully selecting the one she wanted. She turned it over in her hands, running her fingers along the leather, before placing it down on the table again. Once she was happy with her selection, she went to William and placed his hands behind his back, tying them meticulously, just as she'd learned. *Just like riding a bicycle, all of this.*

He smiled, even though it was against the rules, as Addison stood there, admiring him. She grabbed the crop she'd selected from the table. She raised her brow and jutted out her bottom lip. "You like this one, huh?"

He shrugged.

"I need to know you," she told him. "I mean *really* know you," she added, slapping his thigh gently.

William cocked his head and glared at her with a level of intensity she hadn't seen before. "You do know me, Addison."

She shook her head slowly, before trailing her fingertips in and around and underneath his collar. She unbuttoned his shirt, tortuously slow, on purpose. She got to the last button before she spoke. "Do I, though?" she demanded, gently tracing his jawline with her tongue. When she noticed the chills on his neck, she slapped the crop against his pants without much effort behind it. "Why are you seeing Sondra again? And…why do you need this?"

"I don't know," William whispered.

Addison stepped back and paused. "I think you do know."

He sighed. "Sometimes… I just need it. It's a release… it keeps me in control when things get out of hand."

She stepped forward and touched his swollen face. "Do you think you deserve this?" she asked, pressing the tip of her finger to the bruise. He flinched. "Do you think I deserve seeing you like this?"

"No," he said. He looked away and then down at the floor. "I don't know."

Addison tilted his chin so that his eyes met hers. "If we're going to do this, I need to know that I'm enough."

William eyed her up and down and grinned. "Of course, you're enough."

"Fuck," William called out after Addison slapped the crop across his chest.

"I'm serious. Damn it," she said slapping him again.

"Okay. Okay," he said wiggling in the seat. "What is it you're asking for?"

"I'm asking you to trust me to give you what you need."

William frowned. "I do."

She slapped him again, harder this time. "Bullshit."

He eyed her intently. Addison bent over and whispered in his ear, "Is this a joke to you, William? Because I'll leave and come back when you're able to take me seriously. Don't worry… I've got all night."

William inhaled her scent. This was the worst kind of torture. He couldn't take it anymore. He wanted her. "I trust you, Addison. Damn it. I said I trust you."

Addison stood back, she let the hand holding the riding crop fall, and decided to wait him out.

"I don't know what more I can say…"

"Nothing," she said, as she straddled his lap and slowly kissed his chest.

"Funny, you say that. *Nothing* never seems to work all that well with women."

She pulled back. "Fine," she relented. "Say you'll stop seeing Sondra, because I need a man. I need a man who will give me what I need and who'll allow me to give him what he needs. And I think we both know what that is…"

"Okay. I'll stop. Please, Addison. Just untie me," he begged. "I sort of need my hands for this…"

"What's the magic word?"

He thought for a moment. "Mercy," he said. He watched her eyes flicker and he knew he'd given her what she wanted. "Okay, mercy. There I said it… my safe word. There it is."

Addison walked around, untied his hands, and slowly undressed. "Good," she said, pleased. "Now, make love to me."

William was rougher than she'd expected. Rougher than he'd ever been. He pushed her against the wall, shoved himself between her thighs, and pushed into her hard and fast. He waited for her to climax, and then he grabbed her hips and pushed into her harder and slower, relentlessly. It was as though he couldn't get enough, until finally he had. Out of breath, he kissed her face over and over before stopping to search her eyes. "Mercy. *Huh.*" He narrowed his eyes. "I've never used my safe word before, you know."

"Never?"

"No," he said, shaking his head. "But I have to say, it felt pretty good on my lips."

~

ADDISON PICKED THE BOYS UP FROM JESS'S ON SATURDAY afternoon and took them to their favorite Austin ice-cream shop, the one with the shady playground outside, and let them each pick their own flavor.

She watched them carefully, eavesdropping upon their innocence as they ran around with ice cream dripping down their faces. She wished she could freeze that moment in time. She wished that things would always be this sweet and innocent for them, she wished she wasn't about to change everything about life as they knew it.

In the past few weeks, she'd poured over books on how to help children through divorce. In fact, that was what she'd been reading as Patrick packed. Admittedly, a small part of her wanted him to notice, wanted him to beg her to stay, to fight. When he didn't, it only solidified in her mind that this is how it would always be. Even so, the latest handbook on the care of children during divorce didn't help much. It seemed no matter what she did, there was just no easy or one size fits all way to go about it.

Addison intended to feel the situation out that afternoon and finally decided she would tell them in the car on the way home. At first, she thought she and Patrick would gather them together in the living room on the couch and tell them, just as she'd always seen done in the movies. In the end, though, she changed her mind, hoping that she could make it more of a casual conversation than a monumental one. Also, she knew Patrick would never be a willing participant. He would never make it that easy. So, as they piled in the car, sweaty and sticky, she gathered and then almost lost her nerve until Connor spoke up, forcing her hand. "Is Dad going back to China? Is that why we got ice cream before dinner?"

Addison eyed him in the rearview mirror. *He always had been a very perceptive child.* She gathered this was why he'd screamed so much as an infant. Maybe he was simply more sensitive than everyone else. "I don't know, sweetie," she told him, making sure to keep her voice neutral. "But there is something I wanted to talk to you and your brothers about..."

Conner sighed. "I already know," he said. "You guys are getting a divorce."

"What's a divorce?" the twins shouted in unison.

Addison cleared her throat and kept her eyes on the road. "Who told you that, Connor?"

Connor slapped his little brother on the arm. "A divorce is when your parents don't talk to each other anymore and then you get two houses. That's what happened to Lucas's parents, and now he has two bedrooms. He likes it because he says he gets more Christmas presents now—"

"Connor, I asked you a question," Addison interrupted. "Who told you Daddy and I were getting a divorce?"

"Seriously, Mom, I've seen your book," he told her, staring out the window. "I *can* read, you know."

"Oh," Addison said. She bit her lip and glanced in the rearview mirror. "Well, I want to talk to you guys about that. Daddy and I love you all very much, but, you're right, we decided it's best if we don't live together anymore."

"So, we get two bedrooms and more Christmas presents now!" Parker yelled.

"No. I don't know about that," Addison interjected. She pulled the car over, put it in park, and turned around to face toward the backseat. "Do you guys remember when you kept fighting at bedtime and I made you separate and start sleeping in your own rooms and how then I would sometimes find you guys curled up in bed together?"

"Yes," Parker said. "But I sleep-walk."

Addison pressed her lips together and then smiled. "Well,

that's how it is with your dad and me. We love each other, and we love you, but we need to get our own houses so we don't fight so much anymore. In fact, we're going to be moving to a new house in a few days, not far from where we live now."

"What about our beds?" one of the twins asked.

"You can bring anything from home you want, but we'll have new things, too."

"Cool," Parker said. "New toys!"

Addison searched each of their faces. "Do you understand what I'm saying?"

Connor stared out the window. "What about Max?"

"Max is coming with us," she assured him. "Our new house has a big backyard and even a little surprise for you guys."

"What about Daddy?" James probed.

Addison reached for Parker's hand and studied his tiny fingers. "Daddy is staying at home, but you guys can visit him whenever you want. And you'll still go to the same school with your friends."

"Is Kelsey coming too?" Parker asked.

Addison smiled faintly. "She is. And whenever you're ready, I'll take you by and show you the new place."

Connor continued staring out the window as the twins begged to go right this second. Their pleas grew louder and louder.

"Shhh, boys! That's enough." Addison eyed her oldest son. "Connor, so what do you say?"

He shrugged his shoulders, refusing to look at her.

"I know this is hard for you, sweetheart, but I promise—"

"You see that man staring at us?" Connor interrupted, pointing his finger at a car nearby. "He looks like the guy I saw on the news, the one who hurt you."

Addison froze. "Where?"

"Right over there in that car." Connor replied, straining in his car seat.

Addison strained to see a car as it backed out. She grabbed her cell, dialed 911, and put the car in drive. "Boys," she said. "I need you to put your heads down and keep them there until I tell you otherwise, okay?"

She instinctively drove toward the police station as she rapidly fired off details to the 911 operator. "I'm being followed by a man I have a restraining order against," she said hurriedly. "I'm at Lamar and—" Addison paused, suddenly remembering William's security detail would be following her as well.

The 911 operator interrupted. "Ma'am, I need you to calm down and tell me your name. What kind of vehicle are you driving?"

She tried to catch her breath. "Addison. Addison Greyer. I'm in a silver Tahoe. My children are with me." She swallowed hard. "My kids are in the car."

"Okay, Mrs. Greyer, I need you to tell me the name of the closest intersection and a description of the vehicle following you."

Addison's heart raced, and her mouth went dry. "His name is Scott Hammons. The man following me is Scott Hammons," she said, and then she stated her location. "I, uh, I think he's driving a red sedan, a Ford maybe. I'm not sure. I wasn't able to get a very good look..."

The operator spoke slowly and calmly. "I have an officer in route, ma'am. I need you to stay focused on driving. Keep your eyes on the road, hands on the wheel. Breathe. An officer will be with you shortly."

"There's a black Tahoe following me too."

"A Tahoe?"

Addison realized she sounded crazy. "It's the security team—"

"Security?"

"Well—not my security—a friend's," Addison replied, aware of how off the words sounded as they rolled off her tongue.

"Is this security team armed, Mrs. Greyer?"

Addison checked on the boys in the rearview. "It's all right, boys. Everything is going to be okay."

"Mrs. Greyer, I need you to answer my question. Is the security team armed?" the voice in the phone demanded.

"Um, uh, I don't know."

"Do you have a way to contact them?"

"Yes. I can call—"

"Can you give me their phone number, Mrs. Greyer?"

"Let me think.... 512-555-2311. I think that's it."

"Okay, we're letting them know to stand down," the operator said. Nothing made any sense and everything seemed to be happening in slow motion. "Now, do you see the squad car coming up on your right?"

"Yes."

"I want you to follow the officer and pull over when he does, okay?"

"Okay."

"I'm going to stay on the line until you're parked safely, okay?"

"Okay." Addison nodded. "We're pulling over."

"Good. Now, I want you to pay careful attention to his directions, all right?"

"Okay. The officer's here at my window." Addison told her with a heavy sigh. Then she ended the call and reached for the boys.

CHAPTER EIGHT

Patrick arrived at the cabin to find Michele waiting at the table with dinner ready. He studied her sitting there. Michele reminded him a little bit of his mother, but in all of the good ways, of course. She was always ready to just jump in and handle whatever it was that needed handling, and she rarely asked anything of him. Until now.

Driving in, he couldn't help but notice how run-down the place looked since they had been there last, only a few years ago. It was one of the first places Michele took him where they could spend uninterrupted time together. It was so hard back at home, because while they worked together and it was expected for them to be seen around town with one another, they couldn't actually *be* together. This was why, after that first trip, Michele surprised Patrick by buying the place, and they'd since spent many weekends here together "working." Initially, his wife questioned him about it but to his surprise, she didn't press, she knew how much he enjoyed fishing and seemed content when he played it off as a trip with the guys. She'd always been so busy with the kids anyhow, it seemed like she hardly noticed he wasn't around.

Michele stood, interrupting his thoughts. Eyeing the fancy spread, he winked. "Don't you want to try out the bed first?"

Michele took a step forward and kissed his cheek. "Hello to you, too."

Patrick took off his coat and laid it over the chair. As Michele handed him a glass of red wine, he noticed there was something a little off about her; although, he couldn't quite gauge what that something was. "This looks nice," Patrick noted, motioning toward the table.

Michele frowned, glancing at her watch. "Yeah, well, I've been waiting a while, and the food is getting cold. Let's just eat."

Patrick pulled out her chair and sat. "I didn't think you planned to return to the States so soon," he said, digging in. "But I'm really glad you're here."

"I don't want to talk about work, Patrick."

He lifted his brow. "Okay."

"How's the family?" Michele questioned.

Patrick tilted his head. "Oh, you know, same ol' same ol'. The boys are getting bigger by the minute."

She pushed back from the table. "Any plans on leaving anytime soon, Patrick?" She folded her arms across her chest. "Or is this always how it's going to be? You know, just a weekend thing."

"Come on," he said, patting her chair. "Let's just eat. You went to all this trouble. We can discuss that later..."

Michele pulled the tablecloth out from underneath the meal, throwing everything on the floor. "FUCK YOU, Patrick. Is this what I am to you? A fucking side dish? Something you can use whenever you want?"

He stood, wine soaking his pants. "Jesus. What has gotten into you?" He searched the kitchen for a towel and then turned back to her. "Let's just calm down, okay?"

She picked up a dishtowel and threw it at his face. "CALM DOWN? YOU WANT ME TO CALM DOWN? Well, I want you to fucking say something. Say anything. But for goodness' sake, say SOMETHING."

Patrick frowned. He watched her rub at her face as he toweled off. "I am, and I'm saying, 'Calm down, Michele.' Whatever this—this little episode—is about we can work it out."

She glared at him, her face flushed. "Can we? Can we really just work it all out?"

"Let's go shower," he said, reaching for her hand. "It appears we both could use some cooling off…"

Michele's mouth gaped open.

"Please," Patrick pleaded, tossing the dishtowel in with the mess on the floor.

Michele surveyed the meal she'd spent so much time preparing. She shook her head, smiled, and then lowered her voice speaking matter-of-factly. "I'm pregnant, Patrick."

~

AS SHE SAT IN THE BUSY PARKING LOT FULL OF RETAIL STORES and onlookers, Addison contemplated for a moment that maybe she really was losing her mind. She'd given her statement to the officer as quickly as she could. Her children were already understandably frightened, and now, she just wanted to get out of there.

According to the police officer *and* the security team, she'd handled everything wrong. For starters, the security detail hadn't noticed anything out of the ordinary except for the fact that Addison had pulled over to the side of the road. After she'd taken off abruptly, they'd tried to make contact with her car phone, and when she hadn't picked up, they sensed something was wrong. Unfortunately, no one had gotten a decent glance at Scott Hammons with the exception of Connor. Of course, the officer assured her seven-year-olds aren't exactly considered expert witnesses. He took her statement and suggested that given an electronic tracking device was monitoring Hammons they would quickly know whether or not it was him. "Sometimes kids make mistakes," he'd told her. "You know, with their wild imaginations and all."

The problem was, Addison was fairly certain that Connor had not been mistaken. After what she'd gone through at the hands of Scott Hammons, she wouldn't put anything past him. She knew all too well the kind of evil he was capable of.

~

AFTER DISCUSSING THE SITUATION WITH WILLIAM'S SECURITY team and after they'd called in for back up, Addison attempted to keep everything as normal as possible for the boys, and so she did as they'd discussed and took them by the new place to check it out. *Who was she kidding, though? Nothing about any of this was normal.*

She shouldn't have been surprised, though, that once William caught word of the incident he'd taken it upon himself to show up at her new place, which had no doubt caused a huge fight between the two of them. *What was he thinking just showing up here like fucking Superman?* Addison wondered as she pulled him out into the garage. "What in the hell are you doing here?" she demanded through gritted teeth. "Not only are we not supposed to be seen together— but my children are in there."

William threw up his hands. "What do you mean what am I doing here?" he seethed. She watched as he paced the length of the garage. "We're overdue for a meeting. You, me, and the security team."

"I think you're overreacting."

He paused and glared at her. "The hell I am," he said. "We need to get a few things straight. First of all, I need to know what you were thinking this afternoon, not calling Carl—not letting the guys know what was going on. My guys were *right* there, and you called the *police?*"

"That's what you do in these situations, William. You make sure they get documented."

"Which is pretty hard to do if you're dead."

She looked away. "Wow."

He exhaled loudly. "This is getting serious, and one thing is blatantly clear. No matter what did or didn't happen this afternoon, no one was well prepared."

Addison leaned against the wall and crossed her arms. "Look—I . . . I appreciate what it is you're trying to do here, but *now* is not the time."

William stepped forward and took Addison in his arms. "I hear you. I do. I get that you want to protect them. But your thought process is a bit backward."

She backed away and cocked her head. "Don't tell me how to raise my kids."

He held up his hands. "You're right. I'm sorry. I'm trying here. And I do apologize for not calling first, but I needed to make sure you were okay, that you're safe."

"I know. But you can't do this, William. I have children to think about. There's already so much going on. I really *don't* need you adding to it."

"What in the hell is that supposed to mean?"

"It means you need to back off. I can handle this on my own."

William sucked his bottom lip between his teeth and then slowly shook his head from side to side. "You know, Addison, I don't get you. You say you want to try, but you won't let me in. How typical— so long as EVERYTHING is on your terms

—it's all fun and games. I'm just not sure... well . . . I'm not sure I'm compatible with that."

Addison ran her fingers through her hair. "What is that supposed to mean?"

"It means you need to make a decision. We're either going to give this a shot— or we're not. You're either going to let me in— or you're not—because quite frankly, I'm just about done."

"You need to go, William."

William pushed the garage door button and waited as the door slowly rose. Addison watched him walk toward the waiting SUV. He said something to an oversized man as he opened the door for him. William paused before ducking in. He turned back to Addison and saluted her, his face impassive. And then, just like that, as quickly as he'd come, he was gone.

❧

"WHAT DO YOU MEAN YOU'RE PREGNANT?" PATRICK demanded. "I thought you were on the pill?"

Michele glared at him. "I was."

Patrick squeezed at his temples, massaging gently. "Well, fuck. What are we going to do about it?"

"So, all of a sudden you and I are a 'we' now?"

Patrick walked to Michele and put his arms around her. "Come on. Don't be like that. We have always been a 'we.' You know we make a great team."

Michele glanced up at him. "Don't patronize me, Patrick."

This was pretty much the way the conversation went the rest of the evening: back and forth exchanges on how they'd gotten into this mess with no real clear-cut answers as to how to get out of it. Well, he had an idea, but he knew now wasn't the time to ask Michele to get an abortion. He was aware that these things had to be planted, merely suggested, when the time was right. She needed to think it was her idea. He needed time to make her see that it was all for the best. And right now, she was in no mood to hear that. Maybe it was the hormones, but she was on edge. He hadn't remembered Addison being this way. But then, she'd always been a little easier to ignore.

They spent much of the rest of the weekend either in bed or working. Both of them determined to avoid the topic altogether, tiptoeing around it, careful not to set the other one off.

On their last day at the cabin, after making love, Patrick carefully broached the subject. "I think we need to talk about this, Michele."

"By *this*...you mean our baby?"

"Yes." Patrick swallowed. "How far along would you say you are?"

Michele smiled and rolled over, placing her hand on his chest. "I know exactly how far I am."

"All right, well, then what are you thinking?" Patrick asked softly.

"I'm thinking I'm going to have a baby."

"You can't be serious," he said, his tone low. "You know we'll both lose our jobs over this. Don't you?"

She sat up quickly. "I'm dead serious. I never wanted kids, but now, I don't know. It's as though I've been given this opportunity, an opportunity I didn't even know I wanted, and, well, I sort of feel like it's my last shot at it. I'm not exactly young anymore," she told him with a sigh. "And neither are you, for that matter."

Patrick sat up and adjusted the covers. "It's not an opportunity. It's a child. And I don't want any more children, Michele. Don't I get a say in any of this?"

She stood up quickly and sank back down. "Whoa. I'm

dizzy. You . . . You don't have to take part in it," she said, rubbing at her eyes. "I'm fine to do it on my own. Of course, I'd hoped it wouldn't be that way, but if it is, then so be it."

He felt his chest tighten. "What about my job? We're both going to be out of a job after this gets out."

Michele turned and looked Patrick straight in the eye. "I guess that depends, you know? If you want to raise this child together, then I have an idea about how to make it work out for the both of us. But if not— then I guess you're on your own."

~

ADDISON COULDN'T STOP THINKING ABOUT HOW WILLIAM'S arms had felt around her. She remembered how he'd felt inside her. *God, she shouldn't have let him go.* She could still feel his lips on her skin, the way her stomach turned when he touched her. She could still taste him. There was nothing like it. Being with him was like a drug, it put her at ease and yet it made her ache for more. William was a high she knew she'd never achieve any other way. He was her dealer, and she was his addict. *She should have said something, anything, to make him see things her way, to make him stay.*

But she'd known better. The thing about men as powerful as William is that you had to set boundaries with them. They are used to getting their way and without boundaries and discipline, they were nothing. They'd walk all over you; this much she'd learned from her time as a Domme. It was imperative to know when to take it and when to draw the line. As a Domme, it was her job to gauge what it was they needed: how much was too much, how little was too little. With Patrick, she'd lost herself. Patrick wanted to believe that he was the dominant type, but in reality, he wasn't. Her biggest mistake and largest regret was going along with it for so long. She should have put her foot down sooner, disagreed. She should have made him fight. But she didn't. Instead, Addison hated the person she'd become in their marriage. She was desperate for her husband to see her, to love her, to really *know* who she was. She tried ten thousand ways to the sun and back to get him to see what it was she needed. The more she tried, the less he did. After a while, she'd become nothing. Not to him. She was the thing in the room he knew was there but passed without a second glance. The more she strove to get his attention, to become the perfect wife, the perfect mother, the less he saw. In many ways, her marriage reminded her of her childhood, and perhaps there was some comfort in the familiarity.

Part of it was the stress of caring for infants and young children; it became easier not to press, not to push him. There was less energy to go around, and she'd lost the drive to commandeer their relationship in the way she had before. In turn, she allowed Patrick to make all of the decisions about his life, doing as he pleased. While she focused on their home and raising their children and grew more unsatisfied and resentful day-by-day, things for him hadn't really changed at all. If anything, she sat on the sidelines manning the team, while he played the game. She watched as he grew happier in life while she grew more and more discontent. It wasn't that she hadn't wanted to be happy. She did. She just thought if she waited it out, if she didn't demand too much, eventually he'd come around. Turned out, the joke was on her.

It took a long time for her to realize that simply being together didn't necessarily equal happiness. It wasn't until shortly after William Hartman came into her life that it all started making sense. Maybe a part of it had to do with going back to work and hitting her stride again. Maybe a part of it was becoming the confident, assertive Dominatrix Sondra had trained her to be. Maybe she was just playing the part. Even so, Addison knew that most of it was because of how William had fallen for her. It was in the way he looked at her. It was in his touch. It was the way he made her feel when they were together. It was how he drove her crazy. But mostly, it was how he saw in her everything that she should have seen in herself. He called her out on her bullshit. He fought with her and for her. He made her want to be better. But there was a limit to that, she knew.

Maybe she would reach out and apologize. Maybe she wouldn't. Likely, she wouldn't. Addison watched the boys running around their empty new home, laughing and content, and she realized in that moment this was exactly where she needed to be.

~

WILLIAM SAT AT HIS MAHOGANY DESK, THE SAME DESK HE'D once laid Addison across. *God, she'd looked so good there.* He could still smell her on him, could still taste her. And damn him if he didn't wish she were here now so that he could bend her over the edge of that desk, pin her down and spread her legs. He'd show her just how much she frustrated him and yet how much she needed him all the same. He despised himself for feeling this way. He'd had it with her trying to call the shots. *Topping from the bottom, they called it.* Part of the problem was that they were so much alike: stubborn and irreverent.

His current situation was exactly the reason he never got involved with women past a few times in the sack. He hated wanting, or more accurately *needing*, something *so* much. He hated how vulnerable she made him feel. Men in his position couldn't afford to be vulnerable. It was certain death to their persona, which was exactly why he had started seeing

Sondra in the first place. He needed a strong presence in his life, one where he could let down his guard, but still always come out on top. He could take the pain and still come out alive. The risk was measurable. He could survive it. What he couldn't survive was this up and down feeling. He wasn't the kind of man to let a woman mind fuck him into using intimacy as a way to get him to comply with her every whim. It was time to give Addison a taste of her own medicine. William cracked his knuckles and got to work. He was about to teach her a lesson in her own game.

~

For as long as house arrest has been around, people have been circumventing the system. Scott Hammons wasn't exactly on house arrest per se; although, sometimes it certainly felt that way. He was being tracked via his ankle monitor to ensure he didn't disobey the restraining order, which had been put in place.

It had been easy for someone as brilliant as he was to get around under the radar. Even if he weren't as smart as he was, there were products you could find to intercept the GPS tracking device tethered to his ankle simply by typing it into Google for goodness' sake. People were so stupid! Morons. It was his excellent tracking skills—he had been a boy scout after all—that had gotten him closer and closer to his target. Not close enough, but still. He was smart about it. He was an outlier. He always made sure to switch out vehicles and always wore a disguise. Mostly, he made sure to blend in. That was the real trick. That joke of a security team Hartman had surrounding her hadn't seen him. He was that good. And yet, that goddamned kid of hers had somehow managed to foil it all. Now, thanks to the little bastard, his attorneys were breathing down his neck, and the police had questioned him on his whereabouts. But he was no dummy. He knew they couldn't pin anything on him. Scott Hammons was a master at all things. He would show them soon enough.

For starters, he'd understood the art of deflection. He had left the house that day to see his psychotherapist. The damned attorneys insisted on him seeing this idiot, said they'd need his testimony in court. The jury would need to hear that Scott was of sound mind and body. Bloody fucking attorneys! Of course he was in his right mind. He was a goddamned Rhodes Scholar, and no one, especially not bloodsuckers like William Hartman or trashy whores like Addison Greyer, could take that away from him.

William Hartman had humiliated him in front of every-one: the public and even his own family. He should have seen Hartman for what he was: a snake. He'd befriended Scott under the guise of helping him, only to steal his business right out from under him. He'd made a fool out of him. So, while the idiot therapist couldn't understand why he was so angry, Scott knew he had every right. It was his duty to get revenge. Of course, he wouldn't be sharing that with the dummy therapist or idiot attorneys or even that dingbat Penny Greyer; it was his little secret.

Oh, and one other thing he wouldn't be sharing . . . The voices were back.

Well, his wife used to call them the voices, but Scott Hammons had the kind of brilliance to know that it wasn't merely any voice. It was the voice of God. Both God and his angel, to be exact. They instructed him to do their will.

Admittedly, his thoughts had been a bit jumbled recently. He was so busy plotting and planning that there was little time for anything else, even sleep. Also, he couldn't take the meds the doc had prescribed anymore, because with all of this electronic medical record bullshit, it was too easy for the bad guys to see that he was on them again. And he really didn't need the meds anyways. He only took them to appease the doctors and because that's what they said he had to do to win his family back. But he knew better. His angels always informed him in all the right ways, and those meds were poison. He wasn't crazy. He was chosen.

If he were crazy, he wouldn't have been able to see the visions. Only the chosen ones had those powers. Scott stepped back, admiring his handiwork, which was beautifully displayed before him. He had collected dozens upon dozens of photographs of his intended targets, and each day, he paid careful attention to how they were all arranged on the wall. He liked to arrange and rearrange them because God had informed him that this was his riddle to solve.

He'd brilliantly taken all of the photos while he was waiting and watching, save for a few newspaper clippings about the "incident" and the upcoming trial. He also had everything meticulously written down in his journal. His grand plan *had* been to poison his targets, using the very same meds the docs tried to get him to take. He had enough stocked up, enough to certainly do the trick, but then God and his angels played a trick on him and sent him a new vision. They always did like to keep him on his toes. It helped his genius he liked to say. Speaking of genius, his latest vision was crystal clear. He just had to find a red flannel blanket. He didn't have one of those, but according to the vision, it had to be that way. Then he had to find a hill in the woods. At the bottom of the hill in the woods, that's where he would look down and see Addison's body lumped up in the blanket with only her perfect bloody face showing. She'd have a slight smile on her face, which one could still see despite the mess that was now her face, because even in death she would understand that Scott was one of the chosen ones, an angel like the others, and that he hadn't really meant to hurt her. He was only carrying out God's will.

CHAPTER NINE

Dear William,

Have you ever met someone out of the blue one day and suddenly your whole body, every vibrating cell of your being knows that you're supposed to fall in love with the person standing before you?

Your brain tells you differently, so instead of falling into it, you try and ignore your heart's longing, that quiet nagging, the urging that's telling you to go for it. Instead, you listen to the loud wise voice you know to be right in your head. At first, it whispers subtly, "Don't fall in love with this person. He can't love you the way you need to be loved. Neither of you are in a place where love makes sense. The timing is all wrong." Then it becomes louder and louder, and all at once— as if trying to drown out the beat of your ever-racing heart as you stare into the eyes of your lover— it screams at you, "Do not fall in love with this person; it will ruin you." But the trouble is the screams can't— or won't— or simply don't—

drown out what the heart knows to be true. You've already fallen, and you realize then, there's just no turning back.

Looking back, you realize it happened the second your eyes met his. The truth of the matter is what's done is done. Now, all there is left to do is to hang on and enjoy the ride, even if you know it'll lead to your inevitable ruin. "Hang on," your heart says. And so, you do. You hang on with everything you have, with everything you are. You put it all on the line, the good and the bad, because deep down, you know there's simply no other choice to be made.

I love you, William. This is me telling you I'm sorry, in my own way, in the only way I really know how. Yesterday should have gone differently. But there are boundaries we each have set in place for various reasons, and we both need to learn where those boundaries are. Here's hoping there's a better and, more importantly, a more fun way to work out the kinks. ;)

Love,
Addison

Addison settled back into her chair and read what she'd written and then reread it over again. There was so much she wanted to say; she just hoped the letter would convey all of it. She sealed the envelope, dialed the courier with instructions for pickup and delivery, and rushed out to her Monday morning meeting with Jess, who she hoped would make her feel better.

∼

JESSICA SAT THERE NERVOUSLY FIDGETING. SHE DIDN'T KNOW what to expect. She'd only received a few hurried texts from Addison over the weekend, and quite frankly, she was worried about her friend. They'd been so out of sync lately; she never could seem to say the right thing anymore. Sipping her coffee, she took in the hustle and bustle of the coffee shop. There were so many people, so many stories. She took out her pen and notepad and jotted a few things down. Before long, Addison plopped herself down in the chair opposite her. Jess looked up and studied her friend. "No coffee today?"

Addison looked tired. "I already had some," she said, waving Jess off. "If I have any more, I'm pretty sure I'll be able to fly my ass out of here."

Jessica smiled and stuffed her pen and notepad back in her bag. "So," she asked. "How'd everything go with the move?"

"Oh, you know," Addison started to say. She paused to look around the coffee shop. "It's all right."

Jessica eyed Addison quizzically, urging her to go on.

"The new place is great, and we're still getting settled, but the boys seem okay. I'm having one of those play therapists come over this afternoon and spend some time getting to know them."

"A therapist, really?"

"I know. But she came highly recommended, and you're right . . . Maybe it's all a little unnecessary, but I just want to make sure they're really okay. I want to make sure the transition is a smooth one— that they're adjusting."

Jess nodded. "I get it."

"It's all just so much. I know that. And I feel terrible about everything."

Jessica leaned in closer. "Are you all right? I'm really concerned about you. After I got your text about the crazy-guy incident..." she said, pausing to exhale. "I've been so worried."

Addison stared out the window. Eventually, she shifted her attention back to her friend. "I feel like I can't talk to anyone about this Jessica, as though somehow if I say it out loud it'll all be true."

"What will be true, Addison?"

"He's watching me. I know that. I feel it —if that makes sense. Part of me thinks he's just trying to scare me— that he's trying to intimidate me before the trial. But the other part, the other part worries that maybe he's up to more than that."

Jess swallowed hard. "Listen to me, Addison. You need to go to the police. This is serious," she warned. She placed her hand on Addison's arm. "The guy has called you, and now you think he's following you. You just don't mess around in a situation like this, not after, well, especially not after what happened before."

"I have," Addison said, her voice raised. She glanced around, took a deep breath, and calmed herself before continuing. "I *have* gone to the police, Jess. All they do is take my statement and tell me they'll look into it. I don't know what else to do."

"What do the security people say? Do you have any idea why they wouldn't have seen him if Connor did?"

Addison sighed and shook her head. "That's the thing, if he were really there, they *should've* seen him. So, who knows? Maybe he's not really following me," she said, with a shrug. "I don't even know what to think anymore."

"And Patrick? How'd he take it when he got home?"

"About like you'd probably imagine. He's pissed. He called, threatening me with all kinds of legal action. He's picking the boys up from school tomorrow, and then we're meeting to talk after I get off work."

"That doesn't sound *too* bad," Jess replied. She laughed a little and then straightened. "So tell me about the other night with lover boy..."

Addison's eyes flicked back to Jessica. She bit her lip. "What's there to tell?"

"Oh, come on! This is the first time I've seen you perk up in weeks."

"It was . . . It was, well, how it always is—indescribable."

Jess frowned and then pulled out her phone.

Addison studied her face for a second and then spoke slowly. "I know, Jess. I know you think that what I'm doing is wrong. And I don't expect you to agree with it. I could lie and say I can't help myself, but we both know that isn't true."

Jess looked away. Addison went on. "I'm sorry I let you down. I just don't understand why you'd ask if you're just going to make me feel worse about myself. I already feel like shit," she said, her mouth forming a hard line. "Can't you see that?"

"Oh, honey, I'm not trying to make you feel bad," Jess said, inhaling sharply. "Really, I'm not." She looked away and then back at Addison. "I just want to know you've fully thought through what it is you're doing. If anything—I love you dearly— and I just want to make sure you're ready for what it is you're thrusting yourself into. I mean . . . You know men like William Hartman. They're not exactly pillars of success when it comes to relationships and settling down."

Addison crossed her arms and leaned away. "I get what you're saying, Jess. I do. I've thought it myself. A million times. But I love him."

Jess cleared her throat. "That's what I was afraid you were going to say and also why it kills me to have to show you this, but Addison, please, wake up." She leaned in close and lowered her voice. "You want to divorce Patrick? Fine, I support you. But please, really give this thing you're getting yourself into some thought. I'm not sure you're ready for it. That's all I'm trying to say."

Addison took the phone from Jess and hesitantly read the words on the screen.

WILLIAM HARTMAN, ONE OF THE WORLD'S MOST ELIGIBLE BACHELORS, ATTENDS GALA WITH MYSTERY REDHEAD. SAID TO FINALLY BE READY TO SETTLE DOWN.

Addison handed Jess the phone back, stood, kissed her on the cheek. Then she nodded and walked out the door without another word.

~

ADDISON DECIDED SHE NEEDED FRESH AIR AND LEFT HER CAR IN the parking garage near the coffee shop. It was a cold dreary day, especially for a place like Austin. An early cold front had blown through, and even still Texas almost never got this cold. Which is why she hadn't considered the temperature when she'd taken off, but the cold practically forced her to speed walk the few blocks it took her to get to her office. In heels, no less.

Her mind raced. *How could she have been so stupid?* All she knew was that she had to stop the letter from getting to William. Seeing him in the latest gossip rag smiling smugly with a busty redhead draped over him literally made her sick. She'd be damned if she were going to let him make a fool of her. And that's exactly what she was: a damned fool. For so many things, really. For not only believing that a man like William Hartman could love her, but also, for believing that he could be anything other than what he was.

She dialed Carl and asked him to call William's team and

have them intercept the letter. He assured her he'd do what he could only to call her back a few minutes later, his voice solemn. "I'm sorry, Mrs. Greyer. Mr. Hartman has the letter in his possession. He's also asked to see you."

"You tell Mr. Hartman I said that he can go fuck himself," she seethed. She took a deep breath, letting the cold seep in. "In fact, you can tell him that I'm done."

~

WHEN PATRICK ARRIVED HOME TO AN UNEXPECTEDLY MOSTLY empty house, he'd been too overwhelmed by everything that happened over the weekend to really do much about it. Had he not just been forced to swallow the news he had, he likely would've rushed over to wherever his wife was and demanded that she come back home. But now, he wasn't sure that was the right thing to do. Not yet, anyway. He'd dug himself in deep by knocking Michele up; that much was certain.

He needed to talk to his wife. He needed her to make this better the way she usually did, so Patrick cancelled his morning and headed to her office, armed with a plan.

How stupid of him that before now he'd never stepped foot in his wife's place of business. He was so wrapped up in his own world that he hadn't given a crap about what was going on in hers. Patrick knew he'd made mistakes, but he didn't see how things could have gotten this out of hand. After sitting in the waiting room for what seemed like forever, a receptionist ushered him back to his wife's office.

He entered to find Addison on the phone. He sat watching her as she wrapped up the call. The woman in front of him seemed nothing at all like the woman he knew. She looked all grown-up there in that fancy office, using fancy words, in her fancy dress. Patrick wondered how he'd missed so much.

Eventually, she placed the phone in the cradle and eyed him suspiciously. "What are you doing here?"

He looked around the office anxiously. "This is impressive, almost as big as mine."

"I assume you didn't come to check out the square footage."

Patrick cleared his throat. "How did we let it get this far, Addison? I know I've made a lot of mistakes. Trust me. I know that. But we don't even talk anymore. And then you up and move out, just like that?" He looked toward the window and then back at her. "Perhaps I deserve this. I don't know. I just don't want everything that we've worked for to end this way."

She leaned back in her chair and tried to steady her breath. This was just too much: his showing up here, now, like this. She'd already had a shitty morning, and despite the way she felt about him, his words sent her over the edge. "I don't need this right now, Patrick."

He stood and walked over to her, perching himself on the edge of her desk. "Come away with me this weekend, Addison. The way we talked about. We can stay in separate rooms —whatever you want. Please? We'll talk everything over. It's pretty obvious you want a divorce. Okay, I get it. But let's not end on this note."

She traced the rim of her eyelids with her fingertips, clearing the tears. "I can't," she said, her voice earnest. "We'll discuss everything tomorrow night."

"Addison—"

"I need to get back to work," she interrupted, her tone flat. "But—"

The door burst open, cutting her off. "Addison..."

She looked up to see William standing in the doorway.

Patrick stood. "Well, I guess I shouldn't be surprised to see him showing up now, should I? Is that what *this* is all about, Addison? He's in the picture again, isn't he? Which is pretty ironic, given you told me you were finished with this piece of shit."

William lunged toward Patrick as Addison swiftly stepped between the two of them. She placed one hand on each of their chests. She looked back and forth between the two of them and then stopped at William's gaze. "I am," she sighed. "Now— if you'll both excuse me, I *really* do have work to do."

"All right," Patrick said, retreating. "Then, I'll leave you to it." He walked to the door, and stopped. "But, please, give my request some thought."

"I have and I'll come," she replied, so softly Patrick wasn't sure he'd heard her correctly.

~

WILLIAM SAT DOWN IN ADDISON'S CHAIR AND PROPPED HIS feet on her desk. "So," he said, looking at her monitor. "You wanna explain what that was all about?"

She walked over to William and shoved his feet off her desk. "Get out."

"Last time I checked, my name is on the title of this building, and I'm not going anywhere," William scoffed. She watched as he once again propped his feet on her desk. He took up so much space; filling the room, sucking every bit of oxygen out of it.

Addison turned her back and walked to the window.

"I said I needed to talk to you."

"And I *said* to go fuck yourself."

William lowered his voice as he made his way over to

where she stood. "Why are you so angry, Addison? Your letter didn't seem so angry, so—what changed?"

"Fuck you, William," she spat as she tried to back away. Her attempts proved futile. William pinned her in position against the glass effortlessly. She pushed back against him again, harder this time, but it was of no use. His hard body easily held hers in place.

"I asked you a question, Addison. Why are you so angry?"

"I'm not angry," she groaned. "I'm done. There's a difference."

William pushed her harder into the glass. "Is there? Because your body says otherwise."

She smiled and then rammed her elbow into his ribs, gut-checking him. Addison knocked the wind out of him but didn't knock him to the ground as she'd hoped. "Hmmm," she called over her shoulder. "Well, I beg to differ."

"God damn it, Addison." William choked out. "I think we both know what this little episode of yours is about."

She snorted. "And I assume you're here to enlighten me."

William walked to the desk and placed both palms on it, towering over her, looking her straight in the eye. "You saw that BS from the gala and you're jealous."

"Is that all you've got? Because if so, I'd appreciate it if you'd get out and let me get back to work."

William reached over and tucked a loose strand of hair behind her ear, which caused her to flinch. "Nope, you have no idea how much more I've got sweetheart..."

Addison rolled her eyes and then buzzed Sondra, requesting that she come to her office ASAP. William smiled wryly and raised his eyebrows. "Smart girl."

He stood up straight and considered her for a moment. Then he turned to go, but stopped just shy of the door. "Addison, you know... you're lucky I don't just take you right here on this desk. You like to pretend, but I think we both know you want it just as much as I do. Play hard to get all you want, but just so I'm making myself clear, *this*" he said motioning the air between the two of them. "This is far from *done*."

Addison pressed her lips to one another. "Two things you should know Mr. Hartman. One: You're wrong; I'm not the jealous type. I'm the get-even kind. And two: Don't *ever* fucking call me sweetheart again, got it?"

William stood at the door, unable to wipe the smirk from his face as Sondra looked from Addison to William and back again with a fair amount of annoyance.

"You called me in here for this?"

"I was just leaving, actually," William said, glancing at Addison. He liked her angry. He liked her every way.

CHAPTER TEN

William rushed into the elevator and pressed the button. He could feel her coming. He could always sense her proximity. The doors had just about closed completely when he saw the familiar hand slide in between them.

Sondra eyed him from head to toe. "Mind if I ride up with you?"

"It doesn't appear I have much of a choice."

She leaned against the far wall of the elevator and crossed her arms over her chest. "I saw you at the gala with the redhead."

He refused to meet her eye, staring straight ahead instead. "Is that so?"

"*Everyone* saw you, William. What exactly were you thinking?"

William turned to face her then. "Remind me how any of this is your business."

"Remind me how it isn't," she said, cocking her head. "You asked for my help. I helped you, and then you go and fuck it all up. What in the hell is wrong with you?"

"I'm not sure what you mean. Attending an event with a date isn't exactly out of the ordinary."

Sondra sighed and then shook her head. "She's just a girl in love, William, and a naive one at that. She's not used to this lifestyle, *your* lifestyle."

He lowered his voice, made sure his tone was menacing. "And which one would you be referring to?"

"You can have anything when and where you want it. You say jump and people ask how high. Sometimes, I think you forget it isn't like that for everyone else."

William shrugged. "What's your point?"

"You know you're going to hurt her in the end, don't you?"

"Not only is this not your business—but quite frankly, you don't know what you're talking about."

"I know exactly what I'm talking about. My question is why? Why would you choose this? You can't draw her back in and then screw her over. But that's not even the part that *is* my business. I'd like you to explain to me why you talked me into being a part of your plan. Because what you're doing here is a disaster waiting to happen. You know it, I know it, and I sure as hell hope she knows it."

William pressed the emergency stop button. "Look. Not that I need to explain myself to you but I have a pretty good handle on the situation. This *really* is between Addison and me. But . . . if you must know, the redhead was nothing, a decoy to get the press off my back so they'll stop hounding me. And more importantly, her. I'm trying to protect her too; only she's so fucking stubborn, she can't see it. If this is what it takes to get her to see things my way, then so be it."

"You're joking, right? Are you telling me you didn't sleep with that girl? I mean, come on, she was photographed hanging all over you?"

William pressed the emergency button once again, and

the elevator moved upward. "I'm done with questions. Thank you. I am, however, glad to see that you have so much faith in me." He smiled. "Oh, and by the way, Addison says I'm not to see you anymore, so I'm going to have to cancel our seven o'clock. But then you're right, I'm the one calling the shots..."

The doors opened and William stepped off the elevator. He nodded in Sondra's direction.

"William," Sondra called after him, a hint of desperation in her voice. When he didn't turn back, she continued after him, addressing him in a more formal manner. "Mr. Hartman, please reconsider the tactics you're using," she advised, her tone hushed. "It's very obvious what it is you're doing, and it isn't healthy."

William turned and winked. "Says who?"

~

WHEN THREE DOZEN RED ROSES WERE DELIVERED RIGHT before lunchtime, Addison didn't even have to guess who they were from. She knew without a doubt. She sat staring at them for a moment before opening the card. Eventually, she took a deep breath, exhaled, and began reading.

Dearest Addison,

I know you're angry with me, and for that, I'm sorry.

I know you prefer orchids to roses, but sometimes change is nice, don't you think?

You can tell me we're done, if you want. But I know you better.

There is an undeniable magnetic draw that attracts certain people to one another.

It's that way with us, Addison. You can try and deny it, but we're two of a kind, you and I.

Which is why I need to see you. Now.

Carl will take you down through the private exit to the garage and drive you to my place for lunch. I'm already here, so there's no risk of us being seen together.

If you don't come, both literally and figuratively, I'll be forced to keep my scheduled appointment with Sondra this evening.

I don't think either of us wants the second-case scenario. First case always tastes so much sweeter, now doesn't it? And as we both witnessed in your office this morning, coming shouldn't be an issue.

Getting here is more than half the battle. ;)

See you soon.

Yours truly,
William

Addison brought the letter to her nose and inhaled. She could smell him on the stationery, and it infuriated her. She flung the letter down on her desk and searched for her cell. Why? *WHY* did she let him do this to her? One letter, one phone call, the sound of his voice, his scent and suddenly she was reeled back in. Like a moth to a flame, prey caught in a spider's web. That was her. She despised the fact that he was right. She despised the fact there was something about him she couldn't resist. Whatever game it was he was playing, she was drawn to it, and at this point, she couldn't quit even if she'd tried. She knew it, and clearly, he sure as hell knew it. But love, now, that was a different matter altogether. Sure, she'd slipped up once. She knew better than to let it happen again. Lucky for her, no one knew how to wear a poker face; no one knew how to mask love better than she did. No one. Not even William Hartman. She gathered her things. *Game on.*

～

CARL WALKED ADDISON TO WILLIAM'S FRONT DOOR AND offered up a slight smile. "Don't worry, Mrs. Greyer. I can assure you that no one saw us on the way in."

She smiled genuinely. She wanted to tell him that wasn't what worried her at all but thanked him instead. As Carl held the door for her, she inhaled the aromas coming from inside. She made it halfway down the foyer before changing her mind and turning back. She shouldn't be here, shouldn't be giving in to him like this, she told herself before the familiar deep voice interrupted. "Leaving so soon?"

Addison turned and eyed William cautiously. She took him in for a moment before she spoke. Dressed in faded jeans slung low on his hips and a fitted black T-shirt, he looked markedly different from the man she was used to seeing. "Yeah, well, you know getting here was half the battle."

William strode over to where she stood and took her hand. "Stay a while," he said, bending down to kiss her cheek.

She exhaled sharply. "Look, I really can't stay long. My afternoon is pretty hectic," she said, before pausing to look around the living area. "And I just remembered I left my car in the garage around the corner from the office. I gave Kelsey the afternoon off, so I'm going to have to hustle to get back to it after my last meeting as it is."

William pressed his finger to her lips. "Whoa. Whoa. Easy there. Don't worry," he told her. "All of that can be worked out."

"Easy for you to say," she scoffed, walking toward the kitchen. "What is that smell? It smells amazing in here."

William stood back, watching as Addison kicked off her heels. He leaned against the stove, taking her in. "I didn't know what you'd want, so I ordered several things off the menu."

She nodded in the direction of the bedroom. "Like I said, I can't stay long. I've gotta get back, and I really didn't come here to eat."

William rolled his eyes, strode over to where she stood, and kissed her hard. He pulled back, to search her eyes. "All right," he said. "Have it your way, then."

Addison grabbed William's forearm and led him over to the couch where she gently nudged him backward. He reluctantly sat down and then she straddled him. "Don't you even want to talk about why we're over first?" William whispered wryly, slipping his hands underneath her skirt.

"Nope," she replied, slowly unbuttoning her blouse. She made sure her eyes never left his. William smiled as she pulled his shirt over his head.

"Are you sure this is where you wanna start?" he teased, feeling her up.

"Yep." Addison kissed his neck then sunk lower, sucking and biting all the way down to his navel. When he couldn't take it anymore, William swiftly lifted her up off his lap with one hand, quickly undoing his pants with the other. Once he'd pulled himself free, he forced her skirt over her hips, unfastened her bra, and slowly lowered her down onto him. She pushed further. He gasped when she weaved her fingers through his hair and pulled it taut.

He took her by the wrists and held them behind her back as they moved in unison, hurriedly licking and biting at each other until neither one could take anymore.

Eventually William released her hands and took her face between his palms. He kissed her as she blindly searched the floor with her hands looking for his T-shirt. Finding it, she slowly stood and pulled down her skirt. "I've got to get back," she said, tossing it on his lap. "Thanks for 'lunch.'"

"You're fucking kidding me, right?"

She bent down to retrieve her shirt. William took it from her hands. Her eyes met his. "No," she said, taking it back. "I'm not kidding."

"Addison, I didn't invite you here *just* for this. We need to talk."

She walked to the bar and slipped her feet into her black pumps. "Yeah, well, I didn't come here to talk."

William stood and fastened his jeans. "Cancel your afternoon."

"I'm not canceling anything," she huffed.

"I said cancel your afternoon, Addison. We need to talk."

He walked over to the bar and took Addison's phone in his hands. "I'm only going to ask nicely once more. Please cancel your afternoon."

She tried to wrestle the phone from him to no avail. His hands were too big and he was too strong. William picked Addison up in one fell swoop and carried her to a spare bedroom, one she hadn't seen before. "This isn't funny, William. I'm not playing anymore." She laughed nervously as he set her down and cuffed her to a chair. He lowered his voice and then smiled at the sight of her all disheveled and cuffed in his house. "Neither am I."

"Damn it," she said, wriggling. "Seriously." Her tone grew pissed.

William undid a few more buttons on her shirt and then kissed her cheek. "I'm going to go make a few phone calls on your behalf, and then I'll be right back." He winked at her. "You stay put, okay?"

She threw her head back and exhaled. "If you don't uncuff me right now, I swear this is the last time you'll ever see me set foot in your house again."

William laughed and then he slowly closed the door. "Oh, somehow I doubt that."

~

WILLIAM SPENT MUCH OF THE REST OF THE AFTERNOON slowly pleasuring Addison in all the ways she had no idea she'd even liked to be pleasured. He made her beg and plead with him as he brought her to the brink again and again, her anger only making everything he did that much more intense. "See," he said. "You don't get to be in control all the time. I think you'll come to find you like it that way."

"I don't," she assured him.

"Maybe you just need a little more time," he told her.

He introduced her to the arsenal of toys and riding crops he'd bought just for her. Next, he gagged her. "You're going to have to learn to let go," he said. At first, he was careful to keep it on the vanilla side. He could see she wasn't used to being on the other side of the coin.

"Have you never been bound and gagged, Mrs. Greyer?" he asked, trailing the crop along her thighs. When she didn't answer he slapped her with it playfully. She smiled and shook her head. "Is that a no?"

She nodded slowly.

"What a pity," he said, uncuffing her. He led her to the

bed. She went willingly. He was gentle at first. Then he stopped, pulled out, and used his mouth to tease her over and over before he finally bent her over and finished what he'd started.

Eventually he removed the gag. She was spent. She had no idea what was coming next, and he could tell she loved it— whether she was willing to admit it or not.

"You're going to have to learn to let go if this is going to work."

She eyed him quizzically. "Who said anything about making it work? I'm fine with the status quo."

"I'm not."

When she shrugged nonchalantly, he stood, lifted her from the bed and carried her back to the chair, fastening the cuff to the frame. Addison studied him and frowned, but he could swear there was the hint of a smile there somewhere.

She watched as he walked out of the room and came back with a bottle of water. He opened it and held it to her lips. "We haven't done much talking, so I'm not letting you go just yet."

She sucked the water down. "What time is it?" she asked. "I have to pick up my kids."

"I know," he said. "And you will. It's not that time yet."

"You didn't answer my question."

"Carl's going to have one of the guys get your car from the garage and drive it home for you. He'll take you to get the boys in one of my cars to save time."

Addison cocked her head and narrowed her eyes. "William, this has been fun. But I need to go."

He shook his head. "I spoke with your assistant and had her handle your meetings. Everything is fine. You need to stop worrying. Like I said, I've got it all worked out."

"Everything is *not* fine," she said shifting. "Maybe your life works like this—having everyone else handle things for you —but mine doesn't."

"But it can. Do you really think I could be this successful if I did everything myself? No. You have to learn to delegate, to let go of control a little bit."

She watched as William pulled a pair of pajama pants from a drawer and slipped them on. "Yeah well, I'd say I've pretty much given up all control," she told him, motioning toward the cuffs.

"Only because you were forced," he quipped.

After several minutes, he walked over and un-cuffed her. Sitting on the bed, he gathered her in his arms and rubbed her wrists. "Look, I'm sorry about this, but I needed to talk to you, and I needed you to listen."

"This isn't exactly my idea of talking."

"I didn't hurt you, did I?"

She shook her head and scooted herself out of his arms. "No."

"You wouldn't listen before," he said, his face breaking out into a grin. "But you see, you're pretty calm now."

"I have to get my kids."

He smiled. "I checked the calendar on your phone," he told her, glancing at his watch. "You have two hours."

She picked up his wrist and studied the time. "Fine, talk."

William rubbed at his jaw. "I know you saw the photos from the gala, but you could've at least let me explain. You didn't even give me a chance to talk to you."

Addison inhaled slowly and then slipped on the mask she wore well. "What is there to say? You don't need to explain anything to me, William. We're not in a relationship. This . . . This thing we're doing . . . It is what it is. None of that needs explaining."

William, confused, pulled back and studied her face. "I'm

not sleeping with anyone else, if that's what you mean, Addison."

She shifted. "I don't mean anything," she told him. "But you're right. We do need to have boundaries, and seeing you at the gala made me realize that."

"And?"

"And you can do your thing, and I'll do mine. When we're together, we're together. When we're not, well, we each have our own interests."

William stood and ran his fingers through his hair. "Tell me, Addison..." he seethed. "Do you have other fucking interests? Because I don't."

Her eyes grew wide. His face grew red. "It doesn't matter."

"The hell it doesn't."

"We don't have to do this," she told him standing. "Let's not ruin a good thing by driving it into the ground."

William sighed long and heavy. "The girl you saw was there to throw the media off. I figured if they saw me with someone then they'd quit riding our asses and we wouldn't have to worry so much. I was paying her to be seen with me," he said, running his hands through his hair. "Nothing more."

Addison frowned. *Fuck*. Her mask was slipping.

"Mr. Hartman, I'm sorry to interrupt, but we have a situation," a voice called over the intercom.

William stared at Addison waiting for a response. When she didn't say anything, he shook his head. "I'll be right there, Carl."

He started to go but turned back just inside the door. "There's a bathroom right through those doors," he said, pointing to the opposite wall. "Everything you need should be in there, but just hit the buzzer by the door if not. I had your clothes cleaned and pressed, and they're there on a hanger."

She stared at William blankly, refusing to say what was

on her mind. He didn't take his gaze off hers as she entered the bathroom and shut the door. The bathroom was massive, bigger than her bedroom. She considered the time, and then quickly showered and dressed before making her way back to the living area. As she rounded the corner, she heard hushed voices speaking briskly. When she entered the room, it went silent.

William had his back to her and appeared to be staring out the window. He spoke slowly and calmly, his voice rough. "We have to do something," he warned. "This is escalating."

Carl cleared his throat. "Mrs. Greyer."

He turned and exhaled. Addison's heart sunk when she saw the concern written on his face. She glanced from William to Carl to the men she didn't recognize and then back to William. "What's going on?"

William made his way over to her in two swift steps. "Addison, sit. Please."

She took a step back. "Don't tell me to sit," she replied. She turned to Carl. "What's going on here?"

William lowered his voice and ushered her to the couch. "Addison, please." He sat first, and eventually she followed. He took her hand in his. "There's been another incident."

Addison sucked in as much air as she could and still felt as though she couldn't get enough. "Oh my God," she demanded. "Please tell me what's going on."

William closed his eyes just briefly. When he opened them Addison didn't like what she saw. She stood quickly. "I need to pick up my children."

William pulled her back down to the couch and spoke slowly. "The boys are fine, Addison." He spoke calmly, choosing his words carefully. "They're at school, and a team of my guys are with them." She exhaled the breath she'd been holding. William continued. "But, when one of the guys went to pick up your car, what they found was pretty disturbing. We've notified the police, and they're handling it now."

She blinked back tears. "What did they find?"

William squeezed her hand. "Max. He's dead, Addison."

"Max? My dog? I don't understand." She shook her head, all of a sudden feeling faint, like she might pass out. She remembered then that she hadn't eaten. "None of this is making any sense."

William stared at the floor. "They found Max in your car. Based on his appearance, we believe he was killed and placed there."

Bile rose in her throat. "What do you mean his appearance?"

"It wasn't good, Addison."

Her hand flew to her chest. "Oh my god."

"The problem is the garage you parked in doesn't have cameras and isn't monitored."

Addison felt her breath dragging. "No. No. No…"

William watched her carefully. "It's possible that if you'd gone back to your car you could've been attacked."

She rocked back and forth. "Why is he doing this?"

"Hammons is a psychopath," he told her. "I wish I had a better answer for you but it boils down to that. My guys are working with the police to have him arrested."

Addison threw up her hands. "On what grounds? You said it yourself. No one saw anything."

"He won't get away with this, Addison. I promise."

She let the tears spill over. It was too much. "What am I supposed to tell the boys?"

"Is there any way that you and the boys can get away for a little while, Mrs. Greyer?" Carl interjected. "Just until we get this figured out and get Hammons back in jail where he belongs?" Carl interjected.

"I . . . I don't know. I guess. I mean . . . I was going to leave them with my mother-in-law this weekend and go away with their dad. Now, we'll all go," she said, looking up at Carl. "But how long do we need to stay gone? They have school, and I have work."

William coughed. "You're joking, right?"

Addison wiped her eyes with the back of her hand and glared at her shoes.

"Jesus. This just gets better and better," William uttered, before he stood and stormed off toward the kitchen.

Carl took William's spot next to Addison on the sofa. "Mrs. Greyer, I know getting away might be difficult, but it would really be for the best. At least a week would be best, to be honest. Sometimes it helps to diffuse the situation by removing yourself completely."

She nodded understanding the double meaning behind what he was saying. "I don't understand why he's doing this. Why me?" Addison cried, searching Carl's eyes.

"We're going to get him," Carl replied gently, handing her a tissue. "I promise you that."

She stood and smoothed her skirt. "Can you drive me to the school? I need to see my children."

Addison left the apartment and then quickly skipped town, without saying goodbye. And while she never said it directly, William knew she blamed him for what had happened. Hell, *he* even blamed himself, which made him all the more determined to deal with the problem.

～

PENNY GREYER WAS BEGINNING TO WONDER WHY SHE HAD ever decided to help Scott Hammons in the first place. Sure, she despised Addison and of course, she wanted her out of the picture, but she *was* the mother of her grandchildren. Penny worried that maybe Scott Hammons had misread her intentions. Not only that— but she believed he was taking advantage of her. For starters, he hadn't offered up one shred of evidence that her daughter-in-law was up to no good. He said that he'd provide proof, but so far Penny had been the only one doing the providing.

Penny knew Addison was messing around with that Hartman guy again. *Why else would he be providing her round-the-clock security?* What she didn't know was how to get it through her son's thick skull.

She only wanted what was best for her child, which is all any mother wants, really. And unfortunately, yes, she had gone to great lengths— greater than most would have— in order to get her point across—but what else was she to do?

She'd always told Patrick he should've married his ex-girlfriend, and she'd been right. Penny didn't understand what was *so* wrong with arranged marriages. She had it all planned out between him and Sophie, and she knew they cared for one another—at least until that damned Addison entered the picture, that is. No one understood why Penny disliked Addison so much, but what those people didn't understand was having a dream for their child. Hell, Addison hadn't only destroyed the dream that Penny had but she had cost Penny her best friend. When Patrick dumped Sophie and broke her heart, of course Penny's best friend had sided with her daughter without so much as a second thought. So, yes, maybe her hatred of her daughter-in-law was a little extreme, but then again, when you're right about something, you just are. The way Penny saw it nothing was too extreme when it came to protecting one's child.

Speaking of which, Penny had to figure out a way to get herself out of the situation she'd gotten into with Scott Hammons. Ideally, before anyone found out she was involved and everything got worse than it already was. Hammons was proving more and more every day he wasn't stable. Yesterday, he'd surprised her and caught her off guard when he'd asked personal questions about her grandchildren. When she refused him answers, he'd gone ballistic, demanding things she wasn't willing to give, and that was where Penny drew the line. She was beginning to worry that maybe, for once, she'd been wrong. To tell the truth, she wasn't sure if it was that, or Mr. Hammons' unraveling mental state that scared her more.

CHAPTER ELEVEN

Scott hadn't really wanted to kill the damned dog, but sometimes you have to do what you have to do. It didn't help that the angels were angry with him, telling him he wasn't moving fast enough. He could feel the pressure growing more intense by the hour and he hated it when the angels were mad at him. They knew how to make him suffer when they wanted. They made the voices worse. They made them louder. The angrier the angels grew, the louder the voices became, until they were so loud he couldn't hear anything else. *You're not good enough*, they taunted. *You're not smart enough. That's why you're alone and that's why you have nothing. It's all your fault*, they'd chant.

That's why he had to choose something clever, in this case killing the dog, that way they smile upon him and quiet the voices. Thankfully, now that he'd offered up his sacrifice they were happy with him.

But he knew who wasn't happy with him, and that was that dimwit, Penny Greyer. She was growing antsier by the day, more insistent that he show her some proof that her 'little whore of a daughter-in-law' was doing something wrong. While Scott hadn't been able to prove it, he was sure Addison Greyer was seeing Hartman again. He just hadn't been able to get close enough yet, in part thanks to the increased security measures Hartman had employed. But make no mistake— he was watching and waiting— and if he could kill two birds with one stone, so to speak, he was damned sure going to do it. In the meantime, Penny had better get ahold of herself. Apparently, she didn't know who she was dealing with. The angels' anger he could take because he understood their love for carrying out God's will. Penny Greyer, however, was another matter, and the more he thought about it, the more he realized it was probably her fault the voices were getting louder.

Thankfully for him, but clearly not for his intended targets, it was looking as though he was going to officially shake loose of the electronic monitoring bracelet within the next few weeks. His attorneys were pushing to get his trial bumped up and have his name cleared quickly. None of it mattered much to him, as he was smart enough to get around the system anyhow. Not to mention, it was Hartman's security team that was holding him back mostly, not the fact that they were trying to track and trace him. The restraining order was a joke too; one hundred yards was all he had to work with. There was so much you could do from just a hundred yards away. One as agile and brilliant as he was could get in and out without too much effort just as he had with the dog. If only it had been Addison Greyer who'd gone back to her car instead. He so wanted to see the look on her face when she saw her precious pet splayed out like that. He wanted her to see all the blood, the carnage, and to know that he was coming for her next. It's okay, though. He was a patient man and it was all very simple, really. He just had to stay within the shadows, to watch and to wait. The angels assured him it would all play out in his favor. After all, that's the way it works when one is carrying out God's will.

~

THE QUESTIONS BEGAN AS THEY PACKED THE CAR AND THEY hadn't stopped since. Addison stared out the window and watched as the city gave way to country, taking her farther and farther away from where she really wanted to be. Feeling the car closing in around her, she let the window down, sucking in as much air as her lungs could possibly take until she felt as though she might drown. She held her breath and tried to escape the boys' rapid-fire questions. *I thought you and Daddy were getting divorced? Does this mean you're staying together? Why are we going to the lake? What about school? Where's Max? Why isn't he coming with us? It's too cold to swim! What are we going to do there?*

"ENOUGH with the questions, already!" Addison snapped. Patrick looked over at her, pressed the button to raise the window and then placed his hand on hers. *Relax. Everything was fine,* he'd said. *But everything wasn't fine.* She pulled her hand away and leaned her head against the cool, smooth glass of the passenger window. It had only been a few hours and she missed him desperately already. How could she get through the next few days, the next few weeks, or quite possibly the rest of her lifetime without seeing him? Without touching him? She closed her eyes and recalled the words she'd written, unable to get them out of her mind.

Dear William,

Patrick, the boys, and I have gone up to the lake house for a bit, until we figure everything out. I'm sure you already know much of this, but I wanted you to hear the words directly from me, for what it's worth.

I realize that you and I left a lot of things unsettled, but I want you to know that I love you. I love you so much, William. And I'm sorry that life for us has been this complicated. You're right that there is an undeniable attraction between the two of us. You understand what it is I need, oftentimes, before even I myself know what those things are. Still, this has been an uphill battle all the way for you and me, mostly, I believe, in part due to the timing of it all. But it shouldn't be like this. I know you know this, too.

I'm hoping that a little time and space will allow us both to see things a little more clearly. Sure, what we have has been difficult, but it's also been more beautiful than I could've imagined, and that's what I'll take away from it for now. If I've learned anything in life, it's been that love isn't always enough. Maybe there won't be a happy ending for us, but the truth is, I realize now that's okay. It doesn't stop me from still wanting all the beauty that I know life has in store for you. Allow me to say this to you not only as your lover but as your Domme: You deserve so much more than the lies about ourselves that we've been led to believe were true, lies about being unworthy and unlovable and unimportant. If you do nothing else for me, William, do this: Stop. Please, stop believing the lies. They're not true, not a one of them. You are capable of love, of loving, and of being loved. I know, I've seen it firsthand. I also know it's easy to escape into the pain when the going gets tough, because that's what you know. But you're better than that. You deserve to be with someone who takes you as you are because you're beautiful, smart, and generous. I think we both realize I'm not in a place to give you what you need.

Still, you're everything good that there is in this life, William, you and all the parts of you. Going forward, I hope that you'll find and embrace the joy in the pain, in a different, healthier way. More than anything, I hope you know that you are worthy of more. If you won't do it for yourself, then, please, do it for me.

All my love,
Addison

~

PATRICK NUDGED ADDISON AWAKE AS THEY STARTED DOWN THE long gravel drive. How she managed to sleep nearly the entire way was beyond him. Thankfully, it had given him some time to think about what he wanted out of this time with his family. He knew he'd have to tell her about the pregnancy and the fact that he was still seeing Michele. Either he did it or Michele would do it as she'd continuously threatened. In fact, that was the only reason she'd let him get away in the first place. He promised that he would finally tell Addison the truth. And maybe he would. He'd have to eventually anyway, he knew that. But on the off chance that he and his wife still had a shot, he wanted to try. Perhaps it was possible for them to forget everything they'd both done to hurt one another and move on from it. If his parents could do it, maybe they could, too.

It wasn't like he hadn't tried. Patrick had begged Michele to have an abortion, knowing the wrath he'd face due to the pregnancy not only from his wife but also from work and probably most of all from his parents. She refused and had clearly decided she was having this kid with or without him in the picture, which made Patrick wonder if she'd really been on the pill to begin with. In any case, the way he saw it, he was fucked.

"What time is it?" Addison asked groggily, interrupting his thoughts.

He looked over at her. He missed seeing her like this, half asleep, defenses down. "It's after ten…"

"Wow," she said, sitting up, staring out into the darkness. "I pretty much slept the entire way?"

"Guess you needed it. So, what do ya think?" Patrick asked, motioning toward their sleeping children in the back. "Should we wake 'em or carry them in?"

She sighed. "Carry them."

"Just like old times," he said.

She raised her brow but said nothing. Still, he saw it as a win.

Once they'd gotten the boys settled in their beds, Addison put on a pot of coffee while Patrick finished bringing in the rest of their bags. When he returned, he could see that she appeared to be upset and upon further inspection that she'd been crying.

"Is everything okay?" he asked gently.

She rubbed her eyes and headed for the bathroom. "Yeah, I'm just tired; that's all."

"Hey, Addison," he called.

She stopped and turned. "Yeah?"

Patrick exhaled slowly. "I want to apologize for doubting you about this Hammons character. I should've done more, before. But I promise from now on I'm going to do everything in my power to make sure that you guys are safe."

She smiled weakly. "I know."

He waited for her to say more and when she didn't he let out a long heavy sigh. "I'm going to get set up in the guest room; you can take the master."

Addison turned back toward the bathroom, but what she

said next nearly knocked him to the floor. "Actually, I was thinking that maybe tonight you could hold me the way you used to."

"You got it," he told her. Then he picked up his suitcase and headed for the master bedroom, unable to hide the smile on his face.

~

ADDISON QUIETLY CLOSED THE BATHROOM DOOR, TURNED ON the water and let herself slowly slide to the floor. She sobbed until there was nothing left, until the whole of her was emptied out. Then reached for her phone, opened her email, and read through the email once again just to make sure the words she'd read were really there.

From: William Hartman
Date: 01/21/13
To: Addison Greyer
Subject: Mercy

Dearest Addison,

I'm happy you've left town as I think it's the best thing for you and the boys.

After reading your letter, I did some thinking, and as much as I hate to admit it, you are right. It doesn't appear that there is a happy ending for us the way I'd once hoped. I will say that when I heard you'd planned to leave town with him I was furious, wondering how you could betray me, or rather betray *us*, like that. But then the more I thought about it, the more it started to sink in that you'd made these plans before the incident this afternoon with your car, and I think I finally realized that it would always be this way with him. I finally understood that, no matter what, he'll always come first in your life, for no other reason than he's the father of your children.

The more I thought about it, the more I realized that this isn't enough for me. When I want something, I want all of it, and I can see now, that will never be the case.

So, I want you to stay put, Addison. I want you to work it out with your husband, if that's what you want to do. Either way, maybe what happened today was for the best, if nothing else so that we could finally see how dangerous this relationship is for all of us. Also, for what it's worth to you, I want you to know that I do love you, in my own way, I guess. But I would be lying —to the both of us— if I tried to keep up the front that one woman would ever be enough for me. Unfortunately, I'm just not made that way, and while you say that you're okay with it, trying any further would have been disastrous to us both.

William

After a while she stood and washed her face then hopped in the shower and let the hot water wash over her. She knew she shouldn't be so upset. Isn't this what she'd wanted? For him to walk away? If he was going to leave her in the end, didn't it make more sense for it to happen now? It was better just to rip the Band-Aid off and get it over with; she got that. But, if that were the case, then why couldn't she make herself believe the words he'd written were true?

CHAPTER TWELVE

The next few days went by mostly in a blur. The boys were having a blast, fishing and running amok on the property. They'd been blessed with fairly warm weather, which was pretty unusual for January, even in Texas. Addison immersed herself in work, trying to get caught up on everything she'd fallen behind on, in addition to the growing number of leads from the agency. When she wasn't up to her ears in work, she threw herself into her family, going on hikes, and spending as much time with the boys as she could. In the evenings after dark, Patrick would start a fire, and they'd roast marshmallows, sip hot cocoa, and tell ghost stories until it was past bedtime for the boys. Once the boys were in bed, she read while Patrick worked, and then they'd sit and talk for a while about everything and nothing. While it was almost easy to push her incessant thoughts of William out of her mind in the daytime, it was nearly impossible once the sun went down. But even though Addison was heartbroken, she couldn't help but notice how normal it all felt being there, as though if she just tried hard enough, she could pretend everything was okay.

Patrick cleared his throat. "Coming to bed?"

"No," she said, looking up from her book. "I think I'm gonna read for a while."

Patrick walked over to where Addison sat and plopped down beside her. He thought for a moment, choosing his words carefully, before he spoke. "Does this, us being here, seem strange to you?

Addison hesitated. "Yeah. A little."

"Because at times it just seems so normal to me, and then I remember we're getting a divorce," he said matter of factly as though he hadn't rehearsed this exact scenario at least a dozen times. "We should probably talk about that, don't you think?"

"Probably," Addison admitted. She forced a smile.

"What happened between us?" Patrick asked, rolling his neck. "How'd we end up here?"

Addison sighed. "I don't know exactly, but I'd like to think that we're equally to blame."

He cocked his head to the side. "To blame for what exactly?"

"I don't know," she said, setting her novel aside. "I guess we just grew apart. I can't pinpoint exactly when it happened, but we started living separate lives, you know?"

Patrick reached for her hand. "Do you really want this, Addison? Do you really believe there isn't a chance that we could make it work?"

"I think . . . I mean . . . Yes, I do. What we had has been amazing in many respects," she told him looking away. "Just look at the three beautiful children we had together. They're so smart and so much like each of us in their own ways," she added meeting his eye once again. "But they are their own people, you know? That's kind of how I think of us. We were more alike once, but we've changed."

"How so?"

"We grew up, and became less willing to compromise what it is we want."

Patrick recoiled. "What happened with William Hartman, Addison? I need to know the details."

"I don't think that's such a good idea."

"I do," he nodded. "I need to understand."

"I made a mistake," she said, biting her lip. "I slept with him. And then when you left for China, I was so angry, Patrick."

He raised his brow. "Tell me about it."

She shrugged. "So, I just kind of gave into it. I fell in love with him. I never wanted to hurt you. You have to know that. We had just become so distant, and well... I made a lot of really poor choices. I know that doesn't excuse any of them, but I just want you to know that I am sorry. I'm really, really sorry that I didn't handle the dissolution of our marriage better. But I hope you know it wasn't my affair, or even yours, that caused it."

Patrick stood and walked to the kitchen where he poured himself a drink. He held it up. "You want one?"

"No."

"It's surprising, you know. I was really hoping after the past few days that there might be a chance for us."

"I'm sorry," she told him sincerely. "But we're past that point."

Patrick took his seat again opposite Addison. "Are you going to keep seeing him?"

She bit back tears. "I don't know," she said, shaking her head. "I don't think so."

"There's something I need to tell you... Addison."

She pursed her lips. "Okay..."

"Michele is pregnant."

Addison winced. "Oh."

"It's mine."

She shook her head. "Yeah, I think I got that."

"I don't know what to do," Patrick murmured, downing his drink.

"What do you think you should do?" she asked patiently.

"She trapped me. That's what I think."

Addison laughed. "She didn't trap you, Patrick. You trapped yourself."

"Whatever," Patrick quipped.

"Do you love her?"

"I love you."

"Yes, I know. But do you love her?"

Patrick went to the kitchen and poured himself another drink. "I don't know. I suppose."

"Then I think you do know what to do."

Patrick pinched the bridge of his nose. "I need to know there's no chance left for us, Addison. I have to know that I did everything I could to save our marriage."

She softened and gave him what she knew he needed. "You did everything. But come on, we both know this is over. We'll still parent our children together, but as far as our marriage goes, it's over. You can see the boys whenever you want. You can keep the house, but I'm going through with the divorce."

Patrick inhaled deeply and held it.

Patrick frowned. "Whatever you say."

Addison stood, walked to the kitchen, and lightly kissed him on the cheek. "I'm sorry, Patrick," she offered, before retreating to the guest room where she slept like a baby for the first time in a very long time.

~

PENNY GRIPPED THE WHEEL TIGHTLY AS SHE MADE HER WAY TO Scott Hammons' run down place on the opposite end of town. She realized it was time to step away from him after he called her in the middle of the night, furious and demanding more money. When nothing he was saying made any sense, something about angels and such, she finally agreed to meet with him this morning. She promised a check, just to get him to stop calling. The last thing she needed was for her husband to find out about their dealings. Plus, Patrick had mentioned there had been some sort of incident with the police, and though he refused to give any details, because her son was an idiot who insisted on protecting Addison, she couldn't shake the feeling that it had something to do with Scott Hammons.

Penny parked her Cadillac in the drive and stared at the dilapidated house, thankful that she'd never have to set foot here again, after today. What she found inside was disheartening to say the least. Scott had apparently drunk himself into a stupor and she found him facedown, lying in his own vomit.

He was sprawled out on a dirty mattress on the floor, so she nudged him with her foot. When he didn't budge, she nudged a little harder, which caused him to rear up. He sat there for a moment, swaying and then he projectile vomited, which sprayed her shoes.

"Mr. Hammons!" Penny shouted. "What has gotten into you? Is this what you're spending my money on?" she demanded. She picked up one of the many Jim Beam bottles that littered the floor before considering the diseases Scott Hammons could be carrying. She quickly placed it back down.

"What time is it?" Hammons asked as he scrambled to sit up.

Penny had to get out of there quickly, she decided. The stench was making her ill. And the flies were a whole other matter altogether. "I brought your money," she said. "But this is the last of it, Scott. Addison has gone back to my son, and they've decided to work things out. I'm going to let them be for a while... I think it's best for the children," she lied.

"Bullshit," Hammons spat.

"Excuse me?"

He attempted to stand but fell back down, gripping his head. "I'm pretty sure she was with Hartman just a few days ago."

Penny rubbed her chin and thought for a moment before responding. "Well, I don't know about that, but she and my son and the children, of course, are at our lake house now, so I'm afraid your services won't be needed anymore."

"The hell they aren't." Scott slurred. He picked up a bottle, which turned out to be empty. He narrowed his gaze and then he lifted his hand and threw it across the room. Penny took a step back, stealing for the door. She watched as he grabbed a half empty bottle and began chugging it.

Penny placed the check on the table. He really ought to get someone to clean this place up, she thought. "I'm serious, Mr. Hammons. This check will be my last," she warned, careful to keep her tone upbeat. "I do appreciate everything you've done, but we're really no better off than we were when we started." Penny gripped the door handle and turned it.

Scott stood abruptly and grabbed a knife from the table, intercepting her before she could force the door open. Unsteady on his feet, he wielded it in her direction. "Now, you listen," he slurred. "We are NOT finished. You wouldn't want your family finding out what you've done here, would you? You wouldn't want them to know how much money you've given me and what you really think of your daughter-in-law, I'm sure. You think I can't prove that cashier's check has your name written all over it? Tell me how long you think it would be before that son of yours dropped you like a hot potato once he found out, huh?"

Penny held up her hands in protest. "You're right," she agreed, eyeing the knife. "I'm sure we can work something out, but I really must be getting back now."

Scott let out a booming laugh. "You're scared of me, aren't you, Penny? Ha-ha! Look at you. You're shaking."

"Put down the knife, Scott," Penny pleaded.

Scott eyed the knife in disbelief. "Oh, this old thing?" he said, stabbing it into the wall just above Penny's shoulder. "You know I'm really glad we could work this thing out, you and I."

She nodded.

Scott laughed. His breath burned her eyes. "I guess I can expect that I'll hear from you in a few days, then?"

Penny swallowed hard. "Sure," she promised. "I'll call you."

Scott moved over so as to allow her passage to the door. "Not if I call you first." He laughed wickedly.

Penny reached for the handle and turned. This time the door budged. "That sounds wonderful," she said, forcing a smile. Scott stepped aside and let her by.

Penny practically ran to her car as fast as she could. She didn't look back knowing he'd followed her out onto the porch. This wasn't good, she realized. Perhaps she'd underestimated Scott Hammons. He was more than the washed up drunk she figured him to be. He might just be certifiably crazy. She probably ought to tell someone about him threatening her like that.

Penny looked back at the porch. He'd plopped himself in an old recliner. His head hung and she could see that he'd passed out, again. Better yet, maybe she'd just let him drink himself to death. No need to stir up trouble, after all. Men like Hammons always were more bark than bite, anyway.

~

SCOTT SHOWERED AND ATTEMPTED TO SOBER UP. YEAH, HE'D fallen off of the wagon, again. But it happens. He had to stop the voices, so what else was he to do? It's okay, he assured himself. Because now, things were looking up. He had a check to cash and work to do. Damn, that Penny Greyer had pissed him off, which all by itself had been enough of a buzz kill. She was a dumb bitch just like her daughter-in-law, and he'd be damned if he'd let her cut him off like that—toss him to the side— as though he were nothing.

He wasn't nothing. He was brilliant. And because he was brilliant and he had the angels directing him to do God's will, he had a plan in place just as quickly as he'd cleaned up the place a little. He sat down at his computer and got to work, first pulling up Penny Greyer's personal property tax records until he had the exact location where his target was staying. He worked well into the night, mapping, plotting, and planning. He poured out the remaining liquor realizing he needed a clear mind. It was all coming together perfectly. The visions in the woods at the bottom of the hill with Addison wrapped in the blanket all bloodied up from his handiwork made much more sense now that he'd had a chance to thoroughly study the property on Google Maps.

Better yet, for all his brilliance, he realized he now had the perfect little situation right there at his fingertips, practically served up on a gold platter. Garnish included. No one in his or her right mind would suspect *him*, after this. How easy it would be now to frame the husband, the angels whispered quietly. *Think about it*, they'd said. The wife has an affair and files for divorce; the husband plans a getaway to the middle of nowhere, only to have the wifey turn up missing and then later found brutally murdered. Of course! That was it. It was perfect. And now, it was time to get to work, time to dig in and get his hands dirty. His revenge was going to be served up sweet as pie. His decisiveness must have pleased God because He sent the angels to sing him to sleep that night, which was good because it felt nice not to be so all alone.

CHAPTER THIRTEEN

A ddison awoke to sounds of laughter coming from the kitchen. When she saw the bright light pouring in beneath the blinds, she reached for her phone, taking it from the bedside table. She squinted as she checked the time: 9:12 a.m. Addison closed her eyes and smiled. She couldn't remember the last time she'd slept past 7 a.m., much less this late. Opening her email, she scanned through the list settling on her favorite name. She still hadn't responded to William's email and wasn't sure whether she was going to or not. There was something about not replying at all that appealed to her, as though if she weren't a part of the conversation then it wasn't really happening. She clicked on an email from Sondra and was about to respond when her phone buzzed. It was a text from Carl.

Mrs. Greyer, we'd like to request permission to resume providing security. I know that you asked us to stand down during your time away, but we at Hartman Enterprises strongly disagree with that decision. Our team promises to stay out of your way and as inconspicuous as possible. Please, consider it, Addison. — Carl

She thought for a moment and responded.

Thank you for the offer, Carl. But we are fine here.

Satisfied, she clicked her phone off, got up, and headed in the direction of the sound of laughter and the smell of bacon. Following breakfast, she, Patrick, and the boys decided to take a trip into town for supplies.

"They're going to be worn out," Patrick exclaimed, watching the boys run around in a grassy field next to the mostly empty parking lot.

Addison leaned back against the car, folding her arms across her chest, trying to keep the chill out. "One can only hope."

"So," Patrick said, turning to her. "How long are you thinking we need to stay here before the cops can nab this guy?"

"I don't know."

"Hmmm," he said. "Because, I'm a little worried. I've got work and Michele's pretty sick. I called and spoke with the detective this morning, and it sounded to me as though they don't have much on him..."

Addison sighed. "You're free to go if you need to, Patrick," she told him, folding her arms.

"And you, what will you do?"

"The boys and I'll stay on a few more days, just to give them a little more time."

He leaned against the car. "I don't want to leave you guys here alone..."

"We'll be fine."

He shook his head. "Nah, I'm good for a couple more days at least. And, anyway, I think this is good for the five of us."

Addison looked over at him. "Me too," she agreed. "It's good for them to see us getting along."

They spent much of the rest of the day fishing and playing outside. It wasn't until close to dinnertime that

Addison realized she hadn't checked her phone since that morning. There were several missed calls, three from Penny including a voicemail she'd left and two from William. *Why was he calling?* She checked her email. Her heart raced when she saw his name.

From: William Hartman
Date: 01/25/13
To: Addison Greyer
Subject: Call me. It's urgent.

Addison,

I've been trying to get ahold of you all day. Call me. Please.

William

Addison dialed his number then hesitated and hung up. Just as she was about to gather up the courage, her phone rang.

"Hello," Addison said, clearing her throat. She tried to find her voice.

"Addison. We need to talk."

His voice made her dizzy. *God, that voice.*

"Addison? Hello?" William demanded.

"Yeah? I'm here."

She heard him take a deep breath. "Look," he said, exhaling. "I need you to let my men get close."

"Close? For what?"

"For protection. What else?"

She could hear the bitterness in his tone. "William—"

"Look—let me make this simple," he said, cutting her off. "I've had to keep them outside a larger perimeter than they're comfortable with in order to stay off your private property. I need you to talk with your husband… he needs to agree to let them inside the gates."

"I—"

"Where you're at it's just too sparse," he interjected. "They need to be close."

Addison inhaled slowly. "Let me speak. Jesus."

He huffed. "Speak."

"Why are they here? I thought we discussed this... I said we're fine."

"You're not fine."

"You need to tell me what's going on."

William hesitated. "Nothing. I . . . My guys just think it's best until we get a better handle on Hammons and anyone he might be working with."

"What do you mean by 'working with'?" she questioned. Addison heard the uncertainty in his voice. She read between the lines.

"We have reason to suspect that he may not be acting alone; that's all."

"I . . ." she started to say as the boys rushed in.

"Daddy said to come on!" Parker said. "Dinner's ready! Let's go, Mom!" they yelled in unison.

She shushed them away and then pressed the receiver to her ear, hurriedly whispering into the speaker. "I gotta go," she told William.

"Addison this—"

"I said I'd give it some thought, all right?"

"Addison." She heard William say one last time before she pressed the end button.

Hearing his voice was just too much. She sat on the edge of the bed, thought about what he'd said. He couldn't stay in and yet he couldn't let go either. Limbo. It was everything she'd been feeling and then some. This time Addison allowed the tears to fall. *It was time she let herself feel.*

~

WHEN ADDISON AWOKE, STARTLED AND SWEATING IN THE dark, it took her a few seconds to remember where she was. Panting, she fished around the bedside table for her cell phone. She lit up the screen as she fished around with her other hand in search of the button on the lamp. When she found it, she sat up and tried to catch her breath, remembering the way William's face looked in the dream. He was screaming something at her, but his voice was silent. She couldn't hear the words. She rubbed at her eyes, threw her hair in a ponytail and checked her phone again: 1:28 a.m.

Eventually, unable to fall back to sleep, Addison got up, threw on a pair of jeans, and went into Patrick's room. "Patrick," she whispered, nudging him awake.

He woke startled. "Addison? What is it?"

She placed her hand on his chest. "Shh," she whispered, her voice hushed. "It's nothing. Don't worry. Everything's fine. Listen," she said, sitting down beside him. "I need to go back to Austin for a little bit. There are a few things I have to take care of."

"What stuff?"

"Work. I'm going to take the car, but I've emailed your mom and asked her to come up and help until I can get back. The Jeep is here, too, right? In the garage?"

"Yeah," he said, pulling himself up to a sitting position. "But, what time is it?" Patrick asked, shifting.

"After midnight," she told him. "I have to go, Patrick. Please, I need you to not make this difficult…I'll be back later tonight. You need to set the alarm after I leave, okay?"

Patrick sat up straighter and ran his hands through his hair. "This isn't a good idea, Addison."

"It'll be fine," she promised. "I'll be back before you know it. Tell the boys I had to go into work and that I love them."

Patrick sighed heavily. "You're going to see him, aren't you?"

"Yes," she said. "There are a few things I need to get straight."

"Damn it, Addison," he told her, meeting her gaze. "Be careful," he warned. "Our children are counting on you. I'm counting on you.

Addison walked to the door, stopping just inside the frame. "I know."

~

ADDISON TEXTED CARL, WHO WAS WAITING AT THE GATE. SHE asked them to stand down, and begged them not to follow her. Carl refused and only relented when Addison allowed him to ride with her while the rest of the team stayed back at the lake. Recalling the tone in William's voice when he'd called last night, in the end, she changed her mind and let them enter the property, instructing them on how to get into the boathouse. She then sent a text to Patrick, letting him know to expect their presence. She knew he'd be angry, but he was just going to have to deal with it until she got back. When it came to her children's safety, she wasn't cutting corners.

The fact that Carl had insisted on driving only made the trip back to Austin seem as though it took longer. It didn't help that Addison was on edge, fidgeting incessantly. She bided the time by questioning Carl about William. But it was to no avail. He refused, politely, to give anything up. "Just tell me he's not with someone else right now, Carl. That's all I ask—that you don't make me look like a fool showing up unannounced if he's with someone."

"Mr. Hartman is alone at his residence, aside from his

security team and several staff members," Carl replied, keeping his eyes steady, focused ahead.

"None that he's sleeping with though, right?" Addison probed, only half joking.

"Mrs. Greyer, I can assure you that what you're walking into is on the up and up."

Addison nodded and left it at that.

They reached Austin and William's place about an hour or so before dawn. Carl let Addison in. He remained outside as she quietly entered his bedroom. Surprisingly, William wasn't in his bed, forcing Addison to search the apartment for him. She finally found him in his office where she paused in the doorway, taking him in. Dressed in pajama bottoms and a white cotton T-shirt, he looked so peaceful, kicked back in his office chair, his feet propped up on his desk, eyes closed, and headphones in his ears. At first glance, she could've sworn he was asleep, but as she inched closer ever so slowly, he raised his eyelids slightly, quickly sitting up once he noticed her standing there.

William eyed her expectantly. "Addison? What are you doing here?"

"Carl," she said, which she realized made no sense.

He frowned, but then a look Addison couldn't quite discern crossed his face and disappeared as quickly as it had come. "I see."

"It's not his fault," she added, seeing the anger play out across his face. "I forced him to bring me here. I needed to see you... I had a bad dream."

"You're here because of a bad dream?" he asked, his eyes narrowed.

Addison walked over to where he sat. She leaned on the edge of his desk, positioning herself directly across from him. She could tell that was uncomfortable having her so close. She forced herself to meet his gaze straight on. "Yes," she answered. "I mean, no. Well, you see the thing is... I've had this recurring dream for the past several days where you told me it was over between us. The problem is I think you're lying about what you want, and I came here to find out why."

William's jaw tightened. "Damn it, Addison. You shouldn't have come."

She reached for him, but he backed away. "Tell me why you lied. It's killing me, and whether you're willing to admit it or not, I can see that it's killing you, too."

William stood and closed the door before going to Addison. He lifted her a little, forcing her to sit on the desk with him between her legs. He took her face in his hands but he didn't speak.

"I'm right, aren't I? You lied in the email. I just want to know why. I have the right to know, William," she said. "WHY are you lying to me?"

He kissed her hard, catching her off guard. She pulled back and studied his face.

"Because I love you, okay? I love you like I've never loved anyone else. The truth is, I've never really cared all that much about anyone *or* anything else, nothing . . . except all of this." He paused and gestured around the room before continuing. "My whole adult life I've been addicted to this . . . this life-style . . . success, if that's what you want to call it. But you know what?"

"What?" she asked, surprised at his intensity.

"None of it has ever loved me back, until I met you, that is. For the first time in my life, I've wanted something enough to risk everything for it."

"So, you lied..."

"Quite frankly, this scares the shit out of me. You barging in here...I'm not used to having to conform, Addison. I don't do relationships. I'm not good at compromise."

"I don't know what to tell you," she shrugged. "That's how

it works..."

"So they say. Plus—I can't keep you safe. Everything that has happened to you has been because of me. Because of *this.* I can't live without you, Addison. Hell, I can barely breathe without you, but I need to keep you safe. And if staying away from me accomplishes that, then it just has to be that way. I can't explain what it is that you do to me; I just know I need more of it. Being with you makes me feel alive. I'm drawn to you, and I know that what we have isn't what you and Patrick have had or anywhere near that level, but damn it, I want that and so much more with you, Addison. And . . . it kills me to want that, because I know you can't give it to me. You're too good for me *because* you're not like me. You see, Addison, I take from people. I want something, and I just take it without even a second thought as to the consequences. But you . . . You aren't like me. You're incapable of hurting people."

"Stop." Addison interrupted. "You're wrong. You're *so* fucking wrong. I *am* capable of hurting people. I've hurt so many people I don't even know where to begin—my husband, my family, and *you*—but I love you, and I don't know what else to do about it. The truth of the matter is, I probably could live the rest of my life without you. I just don't want to."

William knelt and placed his head in Addison's lap, trailing his face along her thighs, his stubble tickling her tender flesh. "God, you smell so good."

"I missed you," she sighed.

William stood and helped her out of her jacket. "I need to keep you safe, Addison... we have to stop doing this..."

She let him pull her T-shirt over her head and then in one fell swoop watched as he shoved everything off the desk. He took his time with her, covering every inch of her with his mouth. He brought her to the brink, again and again, until she begged him to stop. Then he fucked her, right there on the desk, with enough passion to convince her it possibly could be the last time.

~

THANKFULLY THOUGH, IT WASN'T. LATER THEY MOVED TO THE bedroom where they made love again before falling asleep wrapped up in one another. When Addison woke just before noon, she found the bed empty. She sat up, picked up the robe that was lying next to her, and inhaled William's scent. She pulled it on and went to find him, once again finding him at his desk.

"Hey, sleepyhead," he said with a smile. He didn't look up from his monitor.

"Hey," she murmured as she stood at the window, looking out at the greyness of the day.

"What time do you need to be back? I have somewhere I'd like to take you."

"I probably ought to head out by 3:00 p.m. I'd like to see the boys before their bedtime."

William nodded. "Come here."

Addison turned but didn't move toward him. "When are you going to tell me what's going on? One minute you want me, and the next you don't."

William stood up and closed in on her. "I always want you, Addison. Wanting and having, though, are two very different things."

She sighed, exasperated.

"I need you," he whispered, as he unfastened the robe and watched it fall to the floor.

She removed his hands from her breasts and took a few steps back. "Yeah, well, needing and having are two very different things too, you know."

William grinned. "Oh, really," he said, closing the gap, grabbing her with one arm by her waist, pulling her in. "We'll see about that," he told her, laughing. He wrestled her to the floor.

She toppled him, pinning his biceps to the floor with her knees. "Hmmm," he said, raising his brow. "I could get used to this view," William remarked. He clearly enjoyed letting her win.

She sensed the desperation in his gaze as she trailed her fingers down his chest. "Tell me what's going on, William. I need you to give it to me straight."

"Oh, I plan on it," he told her as he writhed beneath her, feigning a struggle.

Addison lifted her hips and then lowered herself down on him slowly, before pulling up again. "You mean like this?" she asked, sinking lower.

William flipped her on her stomach before she realized what was happening. He pulled her into the position he wanted her in, ass in the air, head down, and gripped one arm behind her back. "No," he replied. "Like this," he groaned, pushing inside her.

He held her in position until they both found their release. Sated and sweaty, William gently urged her all the way down as he hovered just above her. "You make me crazy," he said, his voice rough and hot against her ear.

Addison smiled to herself but remained silent, trying to slow time, trying to remain in the moment. William startled her when he tapped her bare ass with the back of his hand. "Get up, they're waiting on us," he said, extending his hand to help her up. Taking her hand, he led her to the shower where he washed her with such care she wondered how the man standing before her could be the same one who'd just dominated her and left her in a speechless heap on the floor.

As he toweled her off, she swallowed the lump in her

throat and met his gaze with certainty. "The coming and going . . . I just can't keep doing it..."

William smiled but just slightly. "You seem to be doing okay with the coming part."

"I'm not joking," she said, throwing up her hands. She backed away. "I shouldn't have come here. It's not healthy. If we're going to end this, then we need to really end it."

"What is it you want, Addison?" he demanded. "We keep having the same conversation but it goes nowhere. That's not how negotiation works."

"Is that what this is? Negotiation? I thought you said it was over. Wasn't that the point of your letter?"

He shook his head. "I want you safe and happy. That's what this is."

Addison scoffed. "Yeah, well the fucked-up part of all of this is that I only feel that way when I'm with you. Then I leave, and it's like I'm constantly waiting for the other shoe to drop."

William walked from the oversized bathroom into his massive dressing room. He tossed Addison her clean clothes. "I lied, Addison. We have reason to believe that someone is feeding Hammons information about us. He sent pictures of you that prove he's been close. *Too close.* And he knows more than he should for someone who's on house arrest, so clearly, he's either working with someone or he's found a way to beat the system. While we're trying to figure out which one it is, I need to keep you away. Safe. If he or whomever he works with knows that we're seeing each other, it just makes you that much more of a target. I wrote that so you'd stay away."

Addison swallowed hard. "Yeah, well, you can see how well that worked out."

"I need to know if you slept with him, Addison."

She cocked her head. "Slept with who?"

William's jaw tightened. "You mean there's a possibility that there's more than one person I could be referring to?"

Addison flinched as though she'd just been backhanded. "Where are we going, anyway?" she demanded, changing the subject. He'd broken her heart; she wasn't giving him anymore.

William stared at her for what felt like an eternity before he finally spoke. "I know I don't have the right to ask, Addison. Honestly, I'm not even sure I want to know the answer. But I'm going to say this, and this is the last time I'll ever say it. I'm warning you. If you're going to show up here like this, don't fuck with me. I'm not a toy that you can just take out when you feel like playing with it and toss aside the rest of the time."

Addison was pretty sure that's exactly why she'd come here so she could see for herself he'd been lying all along. He loved her. She'd known that deep down. And she had prayed that he would say something to that effect, even if it was in the only way he knew how. *So why then did her victory feel so bittersweet?* She offered up a slight smile, swallowed the words she so wanted to say, and instead offered up the only words someone who didn't want to get hurt again could muster. "Fair enough."

◦⌇◦

WILLIAM HANDED ADDISON A BALL CAP AND WIG. HE instructed her to put them on, that he had a surprise for her as he'd led her to a silver sports car she didn't recognize. It wasn't his, he'd said, not yet, he didn't want it to be traceable to him while they were together, in case they were being watched. But when he'd asked her if she liked it and she told him she did, he'd said that was it—he practically *had* to buy it now. She laughed and suggested to him that perhaps this wasn't the car to take if he planned on being inconspicuous. Maybe they should've taken a Pinto, she'd teased, as he drove her to an indoor gun range on the outskirts of town. The place was seedy and empty. William had rented it out for the afternoon, he told her once inside, after he'd handed her a small handgun. It was a gift for her, a 9mm, and they were there to get her concealed carry permit, he explained before introducing her to a balding man, who would be her instructor.

For the next two hours, she practiced shooting, earning her right to conceal and carry. "I want you to be able to protect yourself," William whispered as he positioned himself behind her, showing her the proper stance. She was a natural, he'd told her once they were back in the car. It was times like these Addison thought she could almost picture them together for real. Times like this when things were so abnormal they almost seemed normal. She never imagined that she'd ever need a gun, but something about being with William just made everything seem different.

William wanted more time. He decided to drive Addison back to the lake house and have Carl follow in her car. After being warned that it wasn't the best idea, William had finally agreed that he'd drive her most of the way and let Carl take her from there. After picking up takeout, they found a scenic overlook and pulled over for a pit stop. They still had several hours drive ahead of them before she was to drive on with Carl but for William, that wasn't enough. "Let's stay for a bit longer," he suggested, after they'd finished eating. Addison checked the time and shrugged. *What could another hour hurt?* William grabbed a blanket from the backseat that they ended up spreading beneath an oak tree. It had turned out to be the perfect winter day, mostly sunny, not too cold and not too hot. They sat there like that for a long while, talking, laughing, and watching the clouds roll by.

Finally, Addison laid her head in his lap. She reached up and touched his cheek. "I almost don't want to go back."

"I know, but you have to, for now." William gently pushed Addison up to a sitting position and eyed her directly. "About that, though . . ." he started and then hesitated before finally going on. "I need to tell you something, Addison, and I need you to promise me—swear to me—that you won't repeat what I'm about to tell you. Not to anyone. Do you understand?"

She swallowed and narrowed her gaze. "William."

"Promise me," he repeated, smoothing the crease in her brow.

"Okay," she relented.

"I'm going to take care of him, Addison. That's why I wrote that. That's why I lied, that's why I need you to stay away."

She threw her head back and laughed but when his expression didn't change, she sat up, and searched his face. "You're joking, right? William, *tell* me you're joking."

William shook his head slightly. "He'll never stop, Addison, not until he wins. Men like him never do. My team is having a tough time getting anything on him, and the cops don't do anything with what they do get. I know what I'm doing, and I need you to trust me. I know I shouldn't be telling you any of this because now you can be implicated should something happen—if it goes wrong. But it won't. And I'm sorry, Addison. I didn't want to involve you in this any more than I already have. But after I wrote that letter, I swear I could almost fucking feel your pain, and it gutted me. When I called, I was going to tell you, Addison. I swear. I was going to tell you what a piece-of-shit liar I am, but I could tell how angry you were with me, and then I heard your boys in the background, calling you to dinner. I thought about you being with him, and I lost my nerve. Lying to you like that, knowing I hurt you and that he was there to ease the pain I'd caused and knowing there was nothing I could do about it, killed me. When you showed up at my place, I thought I was dreaming. I saw the look on your face, and it confirmed everything I already knew. I can't take seeing you hurt like that. I'm sorry," he said before he sighed and looked away.

Addison grabbed his face and kissed him hard. She pulled back as tears sprang to her eyes. "No, William," she begged. "You can't do what it is I think you're planning... I won't let you. Don't you see? You're letting him win. *This* is what he wants. I'm asking you . . . I'm begging you not to do anything stupid. Please," she said, her voice low. "I love you and I need you. You have to promise me."

William watched her face grow more and more serious as her eyes pleaded with his. Finally, after what seemed like an eternity, he leaned in and kissed her forehead. "Silly girl," he chuckled, "you thought I was serious?"

CHAPTER FOURTEEN

Patrick knew Addison would be furious if she found out that he'd invited Michele to the lake. But what was he to do? Michele was furious with him as it was, and she was carrying his child, too, after all. Addison would just have to get over it. So far, though, inviting her there had mostly been a disaster because as it turned out, motherhood apparently didn't come naturally to Michele. She seemed like a fish out of water, uncomfortable and cold. Mostly, she was distant, not too much different from how she was in the boardroom, and it worried Patrick. He finally got up the nerve to mention it after they'd had lunch and he'd set the boys up in the media room.

"Are you feeling okay?" he asked, taking her foot in his hand. "You seem, I don't know, unhappy."

"I'm fine."

Patrick smiled condescendingly. "Are you sure? Because I thought you wanted to be here."

Michele tossed the magazine she'd been reading to the side. "I said I'm fine, all right? What more do you want from me?"

"I don't know, but I was thinking a little interaction might be nice."

She glared at him and then frowned. Next thing he knew, she was standing. Then she stormed off, grabbing her purse from the table. "I'm going."

He stood and took her purse from her. "Don't be ridiculous."

"You want me to sit here and play house, Patrick. That's what you want. Your wife left, so you called me for back up," she seethed. "That's cute," she added, narrowing her eyes. "But I'm not going to do it."

"Come on, Michele," he offered holding his hands up like a hostage negotiator. "I think this is the hormones talking."

She deadpanned. "I think I'm finished playing second fiddle to her."

"Michele…"

"And you know what? Now that I'm having your kid and you're busy acting like one, you suddenly don't seem all that appealing anymore," she hissed.

"I beg your pardon," a voice interrupted.

They turned in unison to see his parents standing there.

Patrick swallowed hard. "Mom. Dad."

His mother turned to his father and then to him. "Patrick? What is going on here?"

Michele squeezed at her temples. "Oh fuck," she whispered under her breath. She took her keys from her purse. "I'm going now."

"Mom, Dad," Patrick said, positioning himself between her and the door. "This is my boss, Michele."

They both stepped forward and shook Michele's hand; they were nothing if not polite.

Once the pleasantries were out of the way, Patrick ran his fingers through his hair. "I thought I told you guys not to come. What're you doing here?" he asked, looking from his father to his mother.

"We wanted to see the children, and we were worried," his father replied, his mouth set in a hard line.

"Obviously, for good reason," Penny chided, fluffing a throw pillow.

"Well," Patrick started before a sudden motion interrupted him in his periphery. He looked over to see Michele falling. He moved in to catch her, but he wasn't quick enough. She landed motionless on the floor. "Call an ambulance," he ordered.

He listened as his parents scrambled. "Mom, get the boys; keep them upstairs."

"It's okay, baby. Everything is okay," he whispered to Michele, over and over as he scooped her in his arms. He rocked her back and forth. "It's going to be all right, I promise," he soothed as blood pooled around her head, and he realized he wasn't quite sure who it was he was trying to convince.

~

PATRICK PACED THE HOSPITAL HALLS AS HE WAITED FOR answers as to what was going on. Michele hadn't regained consciousness, and they were running a battery of tests, trying to determine what was going on. He still hadn't been able to get ahold of Addison. Despite everything that had happened, he was actually pretty relieved his parents had shown up when they did.

It seemed like hours before a nurse finally came out to get him, ushering him into the tiny room where Michele was. She looked different, lying there in a hospital gown, hooked up to so many monitors—definitely unlike the strong woman he was used to seeing.

Suddenly, a tallish man in a white coat appeared from behind a curtain, startling him. "Are you next of kin, sir?" he questioned.

"I'm . . . I'm, um, the baby's father."

The man glanced at the chart and nodded.

"I'm Dr. Patel." He thrust his hand in Patrick's direction, catching him off guard.

"Patrick Greyer."

"Mr. Greyer," he said, looking down at the chart and back up at Patrick. "We're running some tests and haven't found anything conclusive as to why Ms. Raines lost consciousness. She needed a dozen or so stitches, but so far, the scans are clear, and her labs look pretty promising. Right now, my suspicion is that the fainting is pregnancy-related. Dizziness and even fainting is sometimes caused due to the elevation in hormones. The urinalysis shows she's dehydrated, so I've ordered fluids to help with that. It's possible that the dehydration alone was enough to cause this episode, but I want to run a few more tests to rule anything else out."

Patrick sighed.

"Has she been under a lot of stress recently? How about her eating habits? Any morning sickness?"

Patrick twirled the ring on his left hand, the way he always did when he was nervous. "Um, no, not that I know of," he said, realizing how much he actually didn't know about the woman carrying his child. "I mean she mentioned being a little sick, but I think she's eating okay," he replied, running his hand through his hair. He stared at the monitor, silently wondering what all of the various numbers meant. "And the baby? How's the baby?"

"The baby looks great. Everything looks pretty normal at this stage in the game."

He pursed his lips. "Is she going to be okay?"

"After we get some fluids in her, I think she'll perk up just fine. She requested something for pain down in CT, and once everything looked clear, I gave the go-ahead for a small dose of morphine, which is likely why she's out right now. She's going to need to take it easy for the next several days. I suspect after the fall she took that she may have suffered a mild concussion."

Patrick watched as the doc studied the monitor. "By the way, I need to get the name and number of her obstetrician. Do you have it handy?"

Patrick's heart sank. "I, um, I don't know. I guess I can make a few phone calls and find out," he replied, suddenly aware that he should know this. He could see it on the man's face.

The doctor nodded and continued watching the monitors. He stood there for several moments, jotting down notes.

Patrick sunk further in the chair.

"Check the phone," he said, catching Patrick off guard. He moved closer to the curtain and turned to leave.

"Excuse me?"

"Her cell phone. Her doctor's information is probably in it."

"Oh, right," Patrick said, but the man had already disappeared.

~

WILLIAM PULLED THE CAR OFF THE ROAD NEAR THE SPOT where they'd agreed they would say their goodbyes. From there, Addison would travel on with Carl. He put the car in park and killed the ignition. After their previous pit stop, they'd driven much of the way in silence, save for the radio, and Addison had a few things she wanted to get out before they had to go their separate ways. She cleared her throat and stared out the window. "I didn't sleep with him," she said, abruptly. "I haven't slept with him or anyone in months. I don't care if you have . . . I mean . . . I know we aren't in a relationship, but I figured you'd want to know..."

William nodded and laid his head back on the seat, eyes closed. "Why did you agree to go away with him, Addison? Before any of this ever happened with the dog, you'd already made plans. I'm sure you know what that looked like—"

She shifted and turned toward him. "Because I'm scared. My marriage is over, and I hated to see it ending on such a bad note.... but mostly, it's because I'm scared." She drew in a deep breath, let it out, and continued. "I know about your past and why you are the way you are, but the truth is that you know very little about mine."

"I don't care about your past," he said, opening his eyes.

Hers widened.

"I mean, I care. It just doesn't affect the way I feel about you."

"Our past shapes us into who we are. I'm not ready to share all of mine with you, but let's just say that I learned early on not to let my feelings show. I learned that if I wanted to survive, I had to make myself as small as possible and avoid feeling anything. But . . . before I was old enough to figure it all out for myself—if I was sad or happy, depending on what was going on that day—I figured out that I'd better damned sure keep from showing it. If I did, I didn't eat."

"Addison—"

"Wait—" she said, holding up her hand. "Let me finish."

"I was sent to my room to be alone because no one cared enough to deal with the way I felt. People leave, William. They die or they leave. That's what they always told me."

"Yes," he said, trying to add a bit of levity to what she was telling him. "That's typically what happens."

Addison paused and shifted. "I've never shared this with anyone besides Jessica, and even Patrick only knows bits and pieces because it's just too painful, but there's this huge part of me that no one really knows. Maybe that's, in part, because I believe that if they did then they'd somehow see me as less *than* I am."

William shifted. "I don't see you that way, Addison. I see a strong woman, stronger than anyone I've ever met..."

She raised her eyebrows slightly. "The thing is, I've always had this feeling that I wanted to tell you, that somehow I was *supposed* to tell *you.*"

"So do, please."

"All right," she replied, staring out the driver's side window, just past his gaze. She paused to take a deep breath before continuing. "When I was younger, they gave me one of those little potties you use to toilet train your kids with so there would be absolutely no reason for me to come out of my room—"

"They? You mean your grandparents?"

She looked over at him. "Yeah," she nodded, slowly. "Sorry..."

William waited and then urged her to go on.

"Anyway, I'd get thirsty or hungry or maybe just bored, so I'd break the rules. Sometimes I was forced to stay in my room for days, and if I came out, I was spanked for it. Yet, there were many times I didn't even care about getting punished because even though the spankings eventually turned into beatings, they were better than the loneliness. I guess," she scoffed. "It was better to feel pain than nothing at all."

"I can understand that..."

Addison looked away. "A lot of it I was either too young to really remember, or I've just blocked it out. I don't know," she told him with a shrug. "But long story short, I learned along the way that not only did my feelings *not* matter but that I didn't matter. No matter how hard I tried to be what they wanted me to be, I realized it wasn't ever going to be *enough*. In my experience, showing your feelings or having needs got you hurt. And if you're lonely enough or hungry enough, eventually you figure out it's just best not to show it. You learn to deal in other ways. I know that a big part of you understands that—understands what it's like to be this way—but a lot of people won't. I think . . . that unless you've been severely neglected or abused, you can't possibly get what it's like to have to walk on eggshells all the time—to be afraid to show any emotion—to feel so small that you're practically invisible, as if you don't even exist. It's a scary and exhilarating feeling as a child to know that you could walk out the door for school and not come back and that it would be a long time, maybe forever, before anyone came looking for you. Then, before long, you grow up, and it gets a little easier, and you take what you can get, where you can get it. Love is *love*, you tell yourself. You take what it is you feel you deserve, until pretty soon you're lost in it."

William half-laughed. "So, that's what love is…"

"Something like that."

"Really though, what do you think? I genuinely want to know…"

"What do I think? I think it's hard and beautiful and intoxicating because it goes against everything you've ever known to be true. It sort of feels like a lie, but at the same time, it feels though a truth has finally been revealed about yourself. All of a sudden life is different; it's like a high you don't want to come down from. The trouble is—the lows *are* what you know."

"Sounds wonderful," he said, using his teeth to pull on his bottom lip. "And a bit familiar."

She smiled and let it fade. "The good news is, you tell

yourself, if things get rough you *know* how to make yourself invisible. And then it happens. Maybe it's self-fulfilling in that way. But then it happens, and so you play small, in part because it's what you've always done, but also because you're *so* afraid of losing the little bit of love you've worked so hard to earn."

"Why?"

"Why what?"

"Why are you afraid? Because I know what lonely *really* is, and I don't want to go back to *that* place."

"So, you'll do *just* about anything to keep what you have."

"Something like that."

"I don't get it."

"What's to get?"

"I guess I just have a different philosophy is all."

"Enlighten me."

"Everything is replaceable, Addison. No one wants to hear that, especially not women. But it's the truth."

"Hmm…"

"But you're like me," he said, taking her hand. "You don't like to lose."

"Maybe because losing it would somehow mean that they were right about you all along…"

"But they aren't."

William turned and met her gaze straight on. "It's strange, you know, because I knew all of this. I mean somehow, I *knew* it. It's partly what drew me to you that day in the elevator, I think."

Addison laughed. "Insecurity has a scent… is that what you're trying to say?"

"I didn't see you as insecure. Not at all. I saw you as searching for something you hadn't known was missing."

She cocked her head and smiled. "You mean like a job?"

"I mean like an addict. Sort of like how water seeks its own level."

"Sounds lovely," she said, mocking him.

"It sounds like I love you," he countered. "And I think the fact that our pasts are similar is in part why you love me, too. We understand each other. You make me better. *You* make me *want* to be better."

"Like a proper drug."

He twisted his lips. "Everyone has their vices."

"Touché," she said. "But that doesn't make it any less scary when you find one that works."

"What is it that you're afraid of, Addison?"

She exhaled slowly "This," she said, motioning between the two of them. "I'm afraid of *this*. I'm afraid of feeling like this, of getting hurt. I'm afraid of loving you and even more so of *letting* you love me. For a long time, I didn't really understand what happened in the elevator that day. I mean… it didn't make any sense. Having sex with a random stranger."

"It's not that uncommon…"

"For me, it is. Everything I've ever learned is about having self-control. That day, I had none. That wasn't me, and it scared me. Not only did I not even know you but . . . I mean . . . I was happy in my marriage, wasn't I? It wasn't until much later—sometime after the Domme training with Sondra—that I finally got it. I *finally* understood, and I saw myself for what I was—what I am."

William looked confused. "And what's that?"

"Desperate."

"I don't see you that way."

"No," she said. "You wouldn't."

"What happened doesn't make you a bad person."

She sighed. "You see, that's the thing, to a lot of people, it does."

"Who gives a fuck what anyone else thinks?"

She rolled her eyes. "Ninety-nine percent of the rest of the population."

"So that makes it wrong? Because other people think it's wrong? You don't have to let other people dictate the way you feel..."

"No," she said. "But I learned something...I'd been so starved for love, for someone to really want me, to *see* me that I just went with it. And I realized, too, that while the way it happened between you and me might have been a mistake, in many ways, it was also an awakening."

"It wasn't a mistake."

"It split up my family."

William shook his head. "It was a symptom of a bigger problem."

"You should be a publicist...or an attorney..."

"I'm not going to hurt you," he said, cutting to the chase.

"That's just the thing, though. I don't want to find out. We're broken people, you and I. And I think you need . . . I think you deserve someone who's whole."

"Two halves make a whole," he argued. "And I think you're hiding something. I want to know what you're *really* afraid of, Addison."

She shrugged. "I don't know."

"I think you do. But you have to be willing to let your guard down... I want to know the depths of you. I want all of it."

"Fine," she said, biting her lip. "I'm afraid that I *already* love you too much, and I'm just going to get swallowed up in it. I'm afraid of letting what happened in my marriage happen with us. You're *that* kind of man, William. You just eat people up and spit them out."

"And?"

"And, I'm afraid of losing myself again."

"Allowing yourself to be loved isn't losing yourself, Addison. You have to know that."

She shifted and turned toward the window. "What is it you want from me, William?"

He reached over and caught her chin with the tip of his finger, pulling her face toward him. "You want to know what I really want? All right then, I'm going to lay it on the line for you. But you can't leave here and pretend that you don't know anymore. This is it. If I put it out there, you're either going to take it or leave it."

She frowned.

"Do you understand what I'm telling you? No more of this back-and-forth bullshit. If you want to know how I feel —I'll tell you. But once I do, there's no more in and out. You have to trust me enough to let me in."

Addison was caught off-guard by the intensity of his stare. Taking a deep breath, she forced herself to speak. "Okay."

She watched as William smiled briefly before he quickly let it fade away and the intensity in his eyes came back. *She knew that feeling well.* He lowered his voice. "You want to know what I want, Addison? What I want is for us to cut the bullshit and be together. And I mean *really* be together, not this you-meet-me-here-I-meet-you-there kind of thing that we've got going. I want to see our lives unfold together. I want to hold your hand in public. I want people to know you're mine and that I'm yours. I want to hang out with you on weekends. I want to get to know your children. I want to take care of you and let you take care of me in return. But most of all, I want to stop pretending that I don't need you so fucking much. I'm not asking you to spend the rest of your life with me— not *yet*— anyway. But I *am* asking that we decide one way or another where this is headed."

"Okay."

William shook his head and then frowned. "Okay? That's all you're going to say? *Just* okay?"

Addison considered what he'd said for a moment and then she hopped over into his seat and straddled him, taking his face in her hands. "No, not just okay. I love you. I really do, but there are a few things you should probably know about me before you go deciding you want to be with me, *especially* on weekends," she said, feigning shock.

William grinned. "All right then, shoot."

"Well, for starters, I'm not marrying you, probably not ever. And . . . before you decide you want to go and do something as serious as see your life unfold with mine, you need to know that I'm extremely stubborn. I'm hard to handle. Not only do I have difficultly showing my feelings but usually I don't even know what they are."

"Is that all?"

Addison chewed at her bottom lip and then shook her head. "I'm incredibly protective of my children, and if I'm willing to let you in, you have to understand that I'd be trusting you with something that means more to me than anything in this world. You have to promise me that you're not going to fuck that up."

A smile crept across his face. "That's it?" William leaned in to kiss her.

She thought for a moment wondering if there was anything else she should add. Then, she shrugged.

William pulled away and laughed. "Addison, I already knew those things. That's why I fell in love with you. We understand each other. Fuck, we're practically one and the same."

"Promise me you won't do what I think you're going to do."

William cocked his head and reached for her. "And what is that?"

"With Hammons."

"Addison," he warned. "I said I was joking."

"I know what you said, but you also told me you couldn't lie to me, so which is it?"

William lifted her by the hips and ushered her over back into the passenger seat. He stared out the window as though he were unsure how to answer. Finally, he broke the silence. "Do you trust that I love you and that I wouldn't do anything to hurt you? Because I do and I won't. But I won't let anyone else hurt you either."

"That's not enough for me. You have to promise. I need to know that you won't do anything stupid."

"All right," he said. "Let's shake on it." He thrust his hand in her direction, trying to lighten the mood.

Addison playfully took his hand and shook. She glanced toward the windshield. "I don't want to go," she whispered, her expression serious.

"I know," William replied. "This'll be the last time, though," he said, trying to soothe her. It was all he could muster, so he simply held her hand until Carl tapped on the window and told them it was time to move.

CHAPTER FIFTEEN

Penny would be the first to admit that she freaked out a little when she walked in and accidentally overheard that her son had knocked that woman up. *Good God, what was this world coming to? What in the hell had her son been thinking?* She'd certainly raised him better than this. Sure, his father had strayed a few times, but he'd never gotten himself into such a mess.

To make matters worse, Penny hadn't a clue how she was going to pull him out of this one. And it scared her to death to think of what Addison was going to do now. She'd never let him see those children. She'd take everything, there was no doubt. The ball was in her court. There was no pre-nup to stop her because, of course, her son hadn't listened to her when she'd suggested it. That boy was too much like his father to heed any of her advice, and look where it had gotten him. Up shit creek without a paddle, that's where.

Penny had to do something; she just wasn't sure what. Addison hated her, even if she'd never directly said so; there was just too much tension there for her to listen to reason. Maybe it wouldn't matter. Maybe the fall had caused the woman to miscarry. Perhaps all this worry was for nothing, Penny hoped. I mean she didn't really want to wish ill on anyone, but any child that would come into the world under these circumstances would be a bastard, and that was the last thing her family needed. Her mother taught her the importance of upholding one's family's reputation. And really, what did one have without one's integrity? Not much she guessed, knowing full well she wasn't about to find out.

After she had spoken to Patrick, who had masterfully evaded answering any of her questions as to what he intended to do about his little unfortunate situation, she dialed up Scott Hammons. Penny practically begged him to tell her he had something new on that daughter-in-law of hers. He explained that he'd been sick over the last few days but that things were looking up. Also, he was sober now. Thankfully, he sounded clear-minded and rational, because Penny assured him now wasn't the time to play. She advised him that if he could get her some dirt, then it was fine to do whatever he had to do. She'd provide the funding or whatever it was he needed to get the job done. She even suggested he pay someone in Addison's office for information on her; surely someone had to know *something*. She told him to do what he had to do and fast. If he needed more money, then so be it. She would take what she could get. Penny didn't exactly like working with a madman, but what else was she to do? Her family was at risk of crumbling, and what would this mean for her grandchildren? Surely, their mother would take them away, leaving Penny little influence as to how their lives would turn out. She'd even turn them against their own father, Penny surmised.

This kind of thing might happen to other families, but it didn't happen to *her* family. Plus, she could just imagine what they'd all say about her. All of a sudden she would be known as that horrible mother who had raised the son with no values, and it would be as though her entire life, everything she had worked for, everything she had put up with—from the constant need to achieve, to the incessant volunteering, the philandering husband, everything—it would all turn out to have been for nothing—she'd be the laughingstock of the town. *Hey, did you hear what happened to the Greyers?* Life as she knew it would stop. The invitations to parties would cease, and the vacations with friends, all of it, would suddenly disappear. They'd be outcasts, and everything she'd ever worked toward would be for naught. One might accuse her of overreacting, of course, and her husband would likely be one of them, but Penny knew this to be true because she'd witnessed it so many times before. If word got out about this, it would be as though she had been living a lie. People in her circle didn't like liars. Which is why she couldn't and she *wouldn't* allow such a thing to happen. It was time to up the ante.

~

HOT DAMN! HE'D PRACTICALLY BEEN SPOON-FED THE information he needed. Maybe Penny Greyer wasn't so dumb after all. In fact, he was beginning to wonder if perhaps she might be one of his angels in disguise. The good news was that he'd seen the light. He was going to take care of Penny's problem once and for all. All of her problems, too. Not just that little bitch, Addison Greyer. Penny didn't have to tell him that her son was a pathetic philandering loser. Anyone with half a brain knew that just by watching his comings and goings. He also guessed that Penny worried about her grandchildren being raised by such vile excuses for human beings. Since she'd offered to help him and had given him a fresh start—the opportunity to get his own family back —he figured what better way to repay her than to get rid of the daughter-in-law and take the pesky son out of the picture by framing him for murder. If Penny was an angel the way he suspected, it's not like he would be killing her son, only helping her remove the evil from her life. And everyone needed that—angel or not.

Scott knew Addison had been with Hartman; he'd hacked into the surveillance system from the parking garage in his building. One would think that a man with as much money as he had could do better for himself in the way of protecting against these situations, but this *was* William Hartman, after all. That being said, it was time to move. Now that he was sober and Penny was so willing to put a little cash in his pocket, he decided that he'd rather *not* go to trial. There was no need to go through all of that trouble, when he could just as easily let the evidence speak for itself. Once word got out about Patrick murdering his wife, people would know what kind of person Addison Greyer really was. She was a liar and a cheater who had only caused him trouble. People like her weren't worth the oxygen they breathed.

Once he was able to get just a little bit more information out of Penny as to everyone's whereabouts without raising any suspicion on her part, he planned to move in. Most people would make the mistake of striking too soon, but he was smarter than that. If he knew anything, he knew that it was best to wait for just the right circumstance. Luckily for him though, it wouldn't be too much longer.

For now, he simply had to work on getting a little bit closer to the target. The time was near; it was just a matter of throwing Hartman's guys off his trail. They'd been parked down the road from his place for several days now, and although at first, he thought it was the angels watching over him, once he sobered up, the voices settled down enough to allow for his latest vision. He saw that those bastards were keeping tabs on him. Now all he needed was to create a little distraction in order to get out of town. He had the notion that God would be delivering the answer very soon. Soon enough, he would be well on his way.

~

MICHELE WOKE UP AND LOOKED AT PATRICK WITH A CERTAIN resignation he hadn't seen before. "Hey there," he whispered. She looked better than she had earlier; there was finally some color to her face. He reached for her hand and wrapped it in his before she pulled away and ran it down her stomach. "The baby?"

"The baby's fine," he assured her. "How are you?"

She shifted a little in bed and winced, reaching for her head. "Tired."

"I think they're going to let us out of here pretty soon. And I was thinking that since you need to take a few days off, I'd drive you home and stay with you there for a little while —at least until you're back on your feet."

"I don't know, Patrick. I think I'm going to call my sister."

He stepped away and paced the room. "What do you mean you don't know?"

Michele toyed with the IV in her arm, hesitating before she spoke. "I just don't think I can do this anymore. It's not healthy. I mean . . . *clearly.*"

"All right, well, we'll talk about all that when you're feeling better."

"No, Patrick, I think we need to talk about it here. *Now.* This baby means everything to me. I've been given a chance, a gift, you know, and I'm messing it up. I've been so wrapped up in you that I'm not taking care of *me.* Only now, it's no longer about me. Don't you see? What we've had isn't enough for me anymore, now that I have *somebody* else to worry about."

He walked to her bed and knelt down beside her. "I know, Michele. And I'm so sorry. I realize I've been selfish, and I promise you, if you give me another shot, I'm going to make up for it. I don't know how all of this is supposed to work out, but I know now, after everything that happened today, that I want to try. When I saw you lying there like that, I swore to myself, to whoever would listen, that if you were okay then I'd do whatever it took to make it right. So that's what I want. I want to make it right, and I want to start making you happy."

"Oh, yeah? And what about your wife?" Michele frowned.

"I'm going to give her the divorce she wants. Look— I realize that it's what I should've done all along. And I know what you're thinking. I know that I don't have the best track record—but I'm asking you to give me another chance to get it right— if not for me then for our child. Don't you think we deserve to give this a fair shot for *it?*"

Michele wiped tears from her eyes. "For *her*. It's a girl, Patrick… We're having a girl."

His face lit up. "A girl?"

Her smile widened. "Yeah. I had an amnio a few weeks ago… they told me she looks absolutely perfect."

"Wow. So, what do you say? You think we can give it a go?"

Michele grinned. "I say it's time we got you a transfer before corporate has a shit fit."

Patrick climbed in the bed and kissed her forehead gently. He exhaled a sigh of relief, nervously placing his hand on Michele's belly. "Good, I'm glad it's settled then."

～

THE SUN WAS SETTING, AND IT WAS QUICKLY GROWING DARK AS Patrick headed back to the house. He wanted to talk to

Addison before they released Michele from the hospital and explain that he needed to leave for a few days. He still hadn't really gotten a chance to talk to her, but he assumed that she should be back by now. What he wasn't looking forward to though, was dealing with his mother. She and Addison *together* would be pure hell. Still, he figured that Addison couldn't be too angry with him; after all, he wasn't stupid. He knew the real reason that she'd gone back to Austin. That said, he probably should've warned her about the shit storm she would likely be walking into with his parents.

Making his way through the gate, he nodded at the men waiting off to the side in their SUV. It was a different vehicle than before. One that hadn't been there when he'd left, not that he remembered, so he gathered that if they were there now, then his wife was most likely back. He had to admit that having them there was a little strange; he couldn't quite grasp just what kind of person needed to have people following them, knowing their comings and goings at all times. *What kind of life would that be, anyway? What would this mean for his children? How would that kind of lifestyle affect them?* That was something he needed to discuss with Addison. In fact, there were a lot of things that had to be worked out between the two of them. But these talks would have to wait; he needed to get back to the hospital. Sure enough, her car was out front. Taking a deep breath, Patrick stepped out of his car, wrapping his wool coat around him. A front had blown in and the temperature had dropped rapidly from just a few hours before. He put his key in and hesitantly turned the door handle, praying he could get in and get out quickly. Knowing his parents, he guessed not. He tiptoed in and listened for a moment before entering the living area. He shuddered when he saw his parents sitting on the sofa opposite Addison. *This wasn't going to be good.* He looked from his mother to his wife, who was staring at her hands in her lap before she met his gaze. His father cleared his voice and stood. "Patrick."

Patrick retreated. "I don't really have time for this," he said, holding his hands up. "I'm just here to grab a few things. I really need to head back to the hospital here pretty quickly. Addison," he added. "I need to speak to you in the other room, please."

She stood and faced him; oddly enough, he was almost sure that he could detect the slightest hint of a smile upon her face. "Everything okay?"

"Patrick," Penny interrupted. She huffed just once before continuing. "Addison here, assures us that she knew of your situation and tells us that all of this is going to be cleared up amicably, which, of course, we're very pleased to hear."

Patrick looked surprised. "That's always been the plan, Mother—"

"Yes, well your father and I just want what's best for you, but, honey I have to say—"

Penny was cut off as Addison's cell phone rang. She stepped outside onto the deck to take the call. When she came back in a few minutes later, Patrick noticed that her face had drained of any color.

"Patrick, I need to speak to you alone, please," she uttered, her eyes glazed over.

Penny sighed. "I think it's best if your father and I get back home now that the children are in bed. Now that I know everything is okay, we'll leave you two to it. I've got a huge luncheon and still lots yet to put together for it..."

Addison's face suddenly grew red. "Is there anything else you want to tell us, Penny? Anything else you've been working on?"

Penny slung her coat over her arm and stared at her daughter-in-law. "I beg your pardon?"

"How long have you been working with Scott Hammons, Penny? HOW LONG!"

Penny shifted. "I'm sorry," she said, taken aback. "But I'm not sure what you're talking about."

"Mother—" Patrick started.

"Tell him, Penny," Addison urged. "Tell him what you've been up to. Hell, for that matter, why don't you tell us all because . . ." Addison paused to cross the room, placing herself directly in front of her mother-in-law. "Because my sources say that they've seen you coming and going from Scott Hammons' residence."

Penny scoffed. "Well, your *sources* must be mistaken."

"Mother," Patrick demanded. He placed his hands on his hips. "Is what Addison's saying true? I mean . . . Come on, Addison, I really don't think my mother would—"

"Here," Addison said, thrusting her phone in his direction. "You tell me. Does that look like your mom in the photo to you?"

Patrick glanced at the phone and then glared up at Penny. "Well, yeah, *actually* it does."

"Penny, what are these two talking about?" Mr. Greyer finally chimed in.

"It's nothing, okay? *Nothing.* I was just taking him some food."

"Why on earth would you be taking that man food?" Patrick and his father asked in unison.

Penny opened her mouth to speak, but nothing came out. Addison's phone rang again, breaking the silence.

Patrick tried to hear what the male voice on the other end of the line was saying but was unable to make out exactly what was being said. He could only tell that he was speaking in a hurried manner and that the more he said the grimmer his wife's face grew.

"What is it now?" Patrick sighed as he watched Addison make a sudden start for the stairs.

"That was Carl. There's been an incident at the gate with security," Addison called over her shoulder. She spoke rapidly, so rapidly that Patrick was sure he'd mistaken what she'd said. She repeated it once more. "They're advising us to stay inside with the doors and windows locked until further notice."

She made it halfway up the stairs before stopping. "Penny, does Scott know that I'm . . . that *we're* here?"

Penny placed her hands on her hips and stared wide-eyed at her husband, but she didn't reply.

"Mother! This man tried to kill my wife. Now, I don't know what it is you've been doing messing with this man, but this is serious. Damn it! Answer the question!"

"Yes, I think he does," Penny finally relented.

CHAPTER SIXTEEN

Addison made her way into the room where the boys were sleeping. She checked on them, kissed their heads, and covered them up. Although the room was on the second floor of the house, she walked over to the windows and made sure they were locked.

Sliding down to the floor, she pulled her cell from her back pocket and texted Carl.

WHAT'S GOING ON DOWN THERE? SHALL I CONTACT THE POLICE?

She waited, and after a few minutes when there was no response, she dialed William. Her call went straight to voicemail. She was about to dial the police when Patrick quietly opened the door. He came in and knelt in front of her. "Addison," he said, eyes wide. "What's going on?"

She motioned toward the door and then stood quietly, and tiptoed out into the hall. Patrick followed. He leaned against the wall and studied her face. "Addison?"

Finally, she met his eye. "I don't know," she told him,

shaking her head. "I can't get a hold of anyone, and I'm worried."

He frowned. "I'm sure it's nothing," he assured her. "But I really do need to get back to the hospital…"

Addison chewed at her bottom lip. "Your parents said she and the baby are okay. I'm glad to hear that but—"

"They've decided to release her just as soon as someone's there to pick her up," Patrick said, cutting her off.

"Oh." Addison leaned back against the wall and took a deep breath. She checked her phone. Nothing. "I really don't think leaving right now is the best idea…" she said to Patrick. "At least until I get ahold of security and see what the issue is."

The lights flickered and then went out. "What the hell?" Patrick cursed.

Her stomach sank. Addison dialed Carl.

Patrick started for the stairs. "I'll check on my parents and grab some flashlights from the kitchen," he called over his shoulder. "You figure out what in the hell is going on."

When Carl's cell went straight to voicemail, Addison began to panic. She remembered the gun William had given her. It was down in her overnight bag. She ran down the stairs, past Patrick, who was helping his father light candles. As she rounded the corner into the bedroom where her overnight bag was, she noticed Penny out of the corner of her eye, sitting on the couch, her head in her hands. *God, she wanted to kill that woman.* Rummaging around in the dark, with nothing but the flashlight on her phone, she found the bag and the gun. She pulled a hoodie from the bag, it was William's and it smelled like him. She paused for a moment to bring it to her face which she buried it in. Then she threw it over her head and lifted the gun from the bag. She checked the safety, and tucked it in the waist of her jeans. Next, she dialed 911 and willed it to ring. *Nothing.*

She moved closer to the window and tried again. *Still nothing.* It was then that Addison heard the commotion coming from the front of the house. Shoving the phone in the pocket of her hoodie, she started off running for her children but only got as far as the living room when that deep voice she knew so well stopped her in her tracks.

Addison stopped and let her eyes adjust to the candlelight. Suddenly, hyperaware of her surroundings, she noticed Penny pleading with Patrick at the door as the voice spoke again, but it took her brain a moment to process what was being said.

"Do not open the door," she heard him say. "Whatever you do, do not open that door." William urged.

Penny gasped, nodding at Patrick. "Son, we have to. He's killing him."

Addison surveyed the chaos around her. She looked from Penny to Mr. Greyer, who appeared to be trying desperately to dial out on his cell phone. She eyed Patrick. "STOP," she demanded.

She moved between Patrick and Penny and peered out the small window next to the door. What she saw nearly brought her to her knees. Her eyes met William's. He was bloody and beaten, and Scott Hammons was standing directly behind him, holding a knife to his throat. The sight knocked the wind out of her.

Addison instinctively ran her hand along the handgun for reassurance. Then she slowly turned the lock.

"Don't do it, Addison," William pleaded before Scott delivered a blow, which made a horrific cracking sound.

"Okay, STOP," Addison caved. "I'm opening the door," she said, before pausing quickly to turn to Patrick. "I have to open it," she told him, her expression grim. "Go to the kids and take them and hide."

He threw up his hands and narrowed his eyes. "Hide? Where?"

"You know this house better than anyone."

Patrick eyed her with a deer-in-the-headlights look. "I don't think I should leave you."

CRUNCH. Another crushing blow came from outside.

"GO!" Addison shouted, trying and failing to keep her voice calm.

"And what about us?" Penny chimed in. Addison glared at her. Her mother-in-law was wild-eyed and she realized, useless. Addison sighed and then nodded in Patrick's direction. "Go," she managed.

Her father-in-law moved in close. "What does he want?" he asked quietly "Money? We can just write him a check..."

"Somehow, I don't think that'll do the trick," Addison told him, glancing out the side window. She could see Scott pacing.

Once Patrick had cleared the top of the stairs and Penny had started out the back doors onto the deck, Addison slowly turned the lock and opened the door.

Scott thrust William, who could barely stand, through the door. "Hands up!" he shouted, throwing William to the ground. When Addison started for him, Scott kicked William in the stomach. She immediately backed away. "I said, put your fucking hands up!"

Addison did as she was told. Then she watched as Scott took two pairs of handcuffs from his jacket pocket. "You, you little whore," he ordered. "Cuff the old man. Take him to the sofa."

Addison made a move toward her father-in-law. "Wait!" Hammons screeched, lifting a handgun from his waistband. "We're on my time here. You move when I say you move." He pointed at Addison's face.

"Okay," she said, holding her palms up. "Fine."

Satisfied with the fear he saw in her eyes, he continued. "And then… crawl to me on all fours… otherwise your little lover boy here gets tasered again."

She did as she was told but stopped at the sofa. *She knew if she gave him what he wanted now, she was in trouble.* Addison met his gaze dead on. "I'm not crawling to you, Scott," she said, earnestly. "If you want to kill him, do it."

Addison flinched as he placed the taser to William's neck.

"Do what I fucking said!" he demanded. Hammons paused to regain composure. She watched as his expression transformed. "Get on all fours, you little bitch," he ordered her. When she didn't immediately comply, something flickered in his eyes, and Addison watched in horror as William convulsed.

She steadily but slowly moved her hand toward the gun, pretty sure she had a clear shot from where she stood.

"Wait! Stop!" Mr. Greyer pleaded. He shuffled his feet. "Is it money you're after, son?" he added. He glanced down at the floor and then back at Hammons. "Because I can get you whatever it is you need."

Hammons spat. "Does it look like I need money?" he quipped, shaking his head. "You rich fuckers . . . You're all the same—so goddamned stupid. Did it ever occur to you that if I wanted money I would've gotten it from this asshole here?" He hoisted William up, and Addison lost her clear shot. Forcing him to stand upright, Scott demanded William place Addison's arms behind her back. He cuffed her. William trailed his fingers down her arms and when he reached her fingertips he squeezed. She glanced over her shoulder at his bloodied face and swallowed hard.

"Shhh," was all he managed to get out before Hammons was beside them, barking orders. "Where are the others?" he demanded, placing zip ties around William's wrists.

Addison remained silent. "I asked where the others are,"

Hammons hissed, placing the Glock to her temple. "And I'd better start getting some goddamned answers before someone dies here..."

"Okay," Mr. Greyer agreed. His voice shook. "Okay. What—"

"Shut the fuck up—" Hammons interjected. "Look—let's get a few things straight. No one's calling out thanks to this here cell-phone jammer," he told them, waving the device in the air. He laughed and continued. "And no one's going out the gate—at least not in a vehicle anyway—BECAUSE I'VE DISMANTLED THEM ALL. Oh, and those pathetic jokers you call your security team..." he added, waving his hands in the air. "Well, they're indisposed. SO! Hopefully no one's been silly enough to venture outside... because with the temperatures as they are, they'll freeze to death by morning."

"Scott," William said, wincing as he spoke. "Let's handle this like men. Why don't we leave everyone else out of it?"

Scott grabbed William by the hair and sucker-punched him in the face. "You mean like that?"

"Scott," Addison started, and then paused when he sat down between William and Addison on the love seat and placed his arms around their shoulders.

"Did I say you could refer to me by my first name?"

Addison pursed her lips and then scooted away as much as she could before he hugged her back in. "This is going to be so great," he exclaimed to the three of them. "We're all going to become so fond of one another. Sure, some of you are going to have to die," he added calmly. "But the more you're willing to cooperate, the fewer of you that will be."

Addison wondered if she were fast enough to draw her gun and put a bullet in his head. Probably not. But she was willing to try. Only then he shifted and turned toward her. "So . . . tell me," he said before pausing to brandish his weapon. "Where are those beautiful children of yours?"

~

WHAT KIND OF A PERSON WOULD JUST LEAVE HER CHILDREN AND grandchildren in the hands of a crazy man, Penny wondered. Scared out of her mind and out of breath, she forced herself forward, stumbling in the dark. She'd run out the back door so fast that she hadn't even thought to stop to grab her coat. Unfortunately for her, that's also where her cell phone was, in her jacket pocket. It was damp and frigid out, and Penny could barely see in front of her. Still, she continued to put one foot in front of the other. Once she'd gotten as far away from the house as she could, she perched down beside a bush and tried to catch her breath. Shivering, she rubbed her hands together and then breathed into them, attempting to warm herself. Realizing that she needed to figure something out quickly, she weighed her options. She'd either have to make it to the road to try to flag down a passerby or she'd have to get to the nearest neighbor where she could call for help. It was either that—or—she could trek back to the house, which is what she really wanted to do. Only she was well aware that her family was trapped there and that she was their only ticket out. Panting, Penny sank all the way down to the damp ground and considered what it was she should do. Most of the homes in the area were summer homes, which meant their occupants wouldn't be around this time of year. She'd likely have to break in and hope there was a landline available. *This was everything that was wrong with people today,* she thought. No one planned for emergencies. On the other hand, the chances of someone being out on the old farm-to-market road this time of night were even slimmer. When Penny began shivering harder, she realized it was time to move. First, she'd head toward the gate and see what happened to the security team. She gathered she'd find them all dead. At least that was the way it happened in the movies.

Penny didn't know that she'd ever seen a dead body before. *Nonetheless,* she thought, *at least she'd have a good story for her bridge club.* Once she made it to the gate, she'd make the decision about which way to turn.

The drive up to the main house was long, nearly a half a mile, and although Penny couldn't see much, she tried to follow the length of the road while staying far enough off the path that she wouldn't be seen. Every step was a struggle. The wind was biting and she shivered. One minute she willed herself to keep going, and the next she played mind tricks to keep herself from turning and going back. Everyone she loved in this world was back there in that house. Everyone she had worked so hard to protect was now in danger. All she'd ever wanted was to keep her family from the unnecessary evils in life. Yet, look where it had gotten her this time.

~

SCOTT COULDN'T BELIEVE HIS LUCK WHEN HE STUMBLED UPON that shiny car on the side of the road. Back in the day, the pre-William Hartman days, he had been quite the car collector, so of course he would have noticed that kind of car anywhere. Upon further inspection, he'd noticed not only William but also Addison sitting inside. All of a sudden, it was clear that this was a sign from the angels; they'd placed them there on that road for him to see. *After all, what were the odds of that happening?*

He'd worked so hard to evade the men who'd been camped out down the street from his home. Of course, he had to wait until the dead of night and then hightail it out the back door. He'd had to scale three fences and haul ass to the rental car place and then wait six hours for them to open. But he'd done it. Everything had gone according to plan, until now. He had no idea that he could possibly get them so effortlessly, that the angels would hand deliver his targets to him on the side of the road. Scott passed them up at first and then turned around. He parked far enough down the road so that he was out of sight. From there, he traveled on foot along the edge of the woods, just far enough back off the road so as not to be seen. As he sat and watched the two of them there in the car, he considered how he might get close enough to throw off the two members of Hartman's security detail. He just had to move fast enough.

He watched the two of them together, knowing he should move in, and quick. But he didn't. Instead, he finally understood just why he had to carry out his plan. Sure, to the casual observer he hated William Hartman for taking his business, but to someone who paid closer attention, well, that kind of person could see that his hatred ran deeper than that. When Hartman stole his company, that wasn't all he'd taken. He'd taken everything: his livelihood, his family, and his home. He could've replaced the business; he could've built another. Hell, he could have even built another house. But what most people didn't understand was that the son of a bitch had stripped him of every last shred of respect his family had for him when he'd taken his ability to make a living. Scott Hammons was a pillar of success before all of this happened. He'd worked so hard to build the life he was able to afford his family. His children went to private schools, while his wife went to the country club. They went on exotic vacations, while he stayed behind to tend to the business. Sure he missed out on a lot— but everything he did — all of the hours he put in, were for them. It had always been for them. When the business started going downhill, as the profits decreased slowly, the amount of alcohol he consumed steadily increased. They said he burned too many bridges when he was drinking. They said he had a problem, and before long, he found himself voted out of his own company. HIS OWN COMPANY! The company he'd spent years of his life building. Blood, sweat, and tears. All for what? They'd ruined it. They had fucking ruined it—his life's work. First, they staged an intervention and sent him off to rehab, even talked his family into being a part of it; otherwise, he never would have gone. Everything *really* was for them. But did he agree? He did! And what did it cost him? EVERYTHING! They said he was incapable of making sound decisions because he was an alcoholic. But that wasn't the truth, that was just the excuse they used to steal his company right out from under him.

As the money dried up, his wife left and his children stopped calling. But why would they stick around? He hadn't really known them. He didn't even know his own wife anymore. He'd spent most of his life working, working for them. But his children, now grown, no longer needed him, especially now that the money was gone. He'd missed everything. AND FOR WHAT? For a man like William Hartman to come in and take what little he had left? For him to dismantle it and sell it off to the highest bidder? Now, seeing the way he and his little whore looked at each other made him ill. He wanted his wife to look at him like that again. Yes, he might have worked a lot, but he had always, *always* been faithful, not like these two pathetic excuses for human beings. He would do anything just to have his wife look at him like that again. He longed to be the respected businessman he had been once. Now, he was nothing more than a joke. A FUCKING JOKE.

If William fucking Hartman hadn't swooped in to buy up the last of what he had, and in such a public manner—practically proving that his wife was right, that he was a failure—then he would've still had a chance to make it all right. He was *so* close when that asshole ripped everything right out from under him. Now it was time for him to understand what it was like to have everything he loved taken away. Now he would know what it felt like to be powerless as he watched it happen.

Scott sat for nearly an hour until he finally saw movement. A member of Hartman's security, one Scott recognized well, went to the driver's side and, after exchanging a few words, led Addison back to the SUV, and the two of them drove off. The remaining bodyguard climbed into the car with William. They sat for a moment until William exited the car. The huge bodyguard trailed not far behind but stopped at the top of the ditch as Hartman made his way down toward him. He hung back and watched for a minute, not believing his luck. This was his chance. He heard the angels speak, and he knew exactly what it was he had to do. He reached for his gun and took that fucker by surprise, mid-piss. He forced Hartman on his knees and pressed the taser to his neck, zapping him as the bodyguard closed in. Both Scott and the bodyguard had their guns drawn. They stood there for a second in a standoff until the bodyguard slowly started moving in. Once the prick got close enough, Scott took him out with a clear shot to the chest. When the asshole only stumbled, Scott fired another shot, this time aiming for his head. *Bingo.*

Once he cleared the body further into the ditch, stopping a few times to wait for a passersby, he shot the sedative into William's arm just to make sure he wouldn't be much trouble. After Hartman was taken care of, he then continued dragging the heavy, dead son of a bitch until he'd made it just far enough into the woods where his body wouldn't be visible. That settled, he pulled the car down a little closer and wrestled Hartman's limp body into the trunk, which by the way, should be noted was no easy task. And yet, that was only the beginning.

CHAPTER SEVENTEEN

William came to at the sound of Addison's voice. He wasn't sure if it was the beatings, the taser, or the drugs, but he couldn't keep himself from going in and out.

"My children have nothing to do with this, Scott," he listened to her say. "You want to kill me. Fine. Let's go. Let's get it over with…"

No. No. No. William thought.

Hammons laughed.

"That's what you're here for, isn't it?" she continued.

"What do you think?" he said.

"I think," Addison replied. "You should just get on with it."

"Ha. Ha. Ha," Hammons told her with a chuckle. "You think I'm going to make all of this easy for you? The way this bastard made things easy for me? The way YOU made things easy?" he paused and waited for a response. None came. "There's not a chance in hell. Now," he warned. "I think you'd better figure out where that hubby of yours ran off to with those children of yours, because I'm guessing as soon as he hears I'm about to kill his papa he'll happily crawl out from that little hiding spot they're in."

"Scott," Addison said. "This isn't about him, either."

"I don't care," he shrugged. "But oh, what fun we're going to have!"

"Fuck you. If you want to kill someone, kill me."

"Oh, come on," Hammons said, condescendingly. "You of all people should know the art of delay."

"Not really," Addison argued. "What I think... you asked what I think," she said, doing a double take. William willed her to shut her mouth. "I think you're a coward. You like to mind fuck people, but we both know you're all talk. You're nothing more than a drunk..."

William struggled to remain present, to stop Addison from antagonizing a mad man. *He would kill her. He would.* William knew what she was doing. She was trying to protect him. She was trying to save her family and, most importantly, her children by sacrificing herself. Damn him for putting them in the position in the first place. This was his mess to fix, and that's exactly what he had to do, he told himself, as he started slipping again. It was the sound of the slap that jolted him back to reality. William snapped to, and shook it off. When he could, he rose to his feet, and lunged at Hammons only to meet the steel toe of his boot headfirst. The next thing he knew he was being hoisted up and then thrown back against something hard. Eventually, he was drug down a flight of stairs. He remembered hearing Addison's pleas, her begging, screaming for him to wake up. But he just couldn't. No matter how hard he tried, he couldn't will himself back to her. And he knew it was probably going to cost them both their lives.

~

PATRICK WOKE THE BOYS AND HURRIED THEM TO THE GAME room through the patio doors and out onto the deck. They tiptoed down the stairs and across the lawn. He tried his best to keep them quiet, taking turns carrying each of the twins, as he pleaded with them to stop whining about the fact that the ground was hurting their bare feet. He led them to the detached garage and ushered them into the Jeep. It was old and rusty, it hardly ran. Still, he had hope. It was his only shot. Scott Hammons probably hadn't thought to dismantle it, given that it was covered and in the older garage. Or so Patrick hoped. He knew he'd have to push it out; he couldn't risk starting the engine. Not at least until he was far enough out of firing range. In the meantime, he had huddled the boys into the back, on the floorboard. He covered them with an old blanket and ordered them to stay down. He realized he should go back and help Addison and his parents, but he couldn't force himself to leave his children. He decided that if he couldn't get out that he would just have to ram the gate. The Jeep could handle it. He would go for help and hopefully once down the road, he'd finally be able to dial out on his cell phone. He ordered the boys to stay as flat as they could. Then he checked under the hood. Seeing all was clear, he closed it, and put the keys in the ignition. He raised the garage door manually. Patrick did it as slowly and quietly as he could possibly manage but it was still loud. Changing his mind at the last minute, Patrick decided pushing the Jeep out wasn't going to cut it. It was too risky to wait. He'd just have to take his chances, he thought as he revved the engine and pushed the gas pedal full throttle.

～

Damn it. Damn it. Damn it. Clearly, Scott reminded himself, he hadn't thought this through very well, and the angels were angry with him. The voices in his head were growing louder, and he didn't know what he was supposed to do to shut them up. They had to stop; he couldn't think straight with them shouting and scrambling his thoughts this way. He knew the only way to silence them was to give them what they wanted. They wanted a sacrifice. And in order to please them, he realized it meant that everyone had to die, even the children, which was a pity, but what could he do?

The old man was handcuffed and tied to the pillar in the living room. And damn if he didn't keep complaining of chest pains. But Scott was too brilliant a man to fall for that. Based on the annoyance factor alone, it was clear the old man would have to be the first to die. He'd shoot him first, and then he'd kill the whore. Lastly, he'd finish off Hartman, who by the look of things was already halfway there.

Once he'd taken care of business, he'd set the house on fire, destroying any evidence of him having been there at all. If they did suspect him, now that Penny had gotten away, well, they'd just think he burned in the fire with the rest of them. Plus, she probably wouldn't make it through the night in that type of weather, anyhow. He'd have to eventually go out to the garage to collect the gasoline he'd need to do the job, but first he wanted a drink. After all this, he deserved that much. He poured himself a scotch, kicked it back, and then poured another. He'd just lifted the bottle to fill his glass once again when he heard the roar of the engine outside. *Motherfucker!* Dropping the bottle, he bolted toward the front door and peeked outside. He watched as the taillights began to fade into the dark. *This wasn't happening. It was the voices.* Scott threw open the door and ran full force in the direction of the vehicle and drew his gun, firing off a few rounds. He aimed for the tires and emptied his chamber. He wasn't very effective, likely on account of the scotch. Mostly, he missed as the Jeep swerved back and forth, in an attempt to try and evade his shots. *His father had been right.* He always told him, it's hard to hit a moving target. Scott watched as the taillights faded in the distance. *God damn it!* That was it. He had to finish this thing now. The clock was running, and it was time he got on with it.

~

Addison huddled next to William in the wine cellar. She watched the rise and fall of his chest and counted the way she had when the boys were babies, back when she'd checked nearly every few minutes to make sure they were still breathing. Gently nudging him with her foot, Addison called for him to wake up. She figured, at best, she only had a few minutes to make this work. Hammons had slapped her around quite a bit and terrorized the two of them for what felt like hours, but for the most part, she was still okay. Unlike William. She hoped Patrick had made it out with the boys. She begged to whatever God that would listen that if he'd just get them out alive then he could take her. That's all she wanted. *Please God.* Addison prayed over and over to herself. *Just get them out. They had to get out.*

"William," she whispered. "William!"

Finally, he lifted his eyelids. Just barely. He moaned.

"William. We're going to die here if you don't help me. I need you to wake up," she pleaded. "God..." she panicked. "Please wake up."

He tried to speak. Everything was garbled. Incoherent.

"William? Can you hear me?"

Wincing, he raised his eyebrows ever so slightly.

"William! I have *the* gun," Addison told him. "But my hands are tied."

He opened the eye that wasn't swollen shut.

"I'm going to back myself up to your hands as best I can, and you have to reach into my pants and pull it out, okay? And then I want you to hand it to me..."

William shifted.

She scooted closer. "NO," she told him. "I want you to stay put."

He cocked his head.

"Stay put," she told him once again. "I'm coming to you."

She moved closer until she felt his hands on her thighs.

"All right," she said, relieved. "Now move your hands upward slowly. If we drop it, we're fucked. So just go slowly."

Addison watched his hand slide slowly up her thigh. He reached just inside the waist of her pants and removed the gun. She eyed William cautiously. "Okay," she whispered. "Now hand it to me."

Only he didn't budge, and he didn't open his eyes. He held the gun tightly. "No, Addison," he told her finally. "I got this."

She gritted her teeth. "You don't have this, William," she said, dropping her tone. "You don't fucking have it. You can barely keep your eyes open," she told him. "Now give me the gun. I can do it."

He opened his left eye. "I need you to trust me," he countered. "I'm not opening my eyes because I'm conserving my energy, but I'm an expert marksman. You do realize that you'd have to shoot with your hands tied behind your back, don't you?"

"So? At least I'm not going in and out of consciousness. Who knows when he'll be back..."

"Look at me. I'm in such bad shape he won't expect much."

Addison rolled her eyes. "Conserving energy, my ass," she hissed. "I'm not betting my life on this. William, give me the gun!"

She watched as he clicked the safety off and slowly, painfully rolled all the way onto his back, covering the gun with his body.

Addison inhaled as she heard the door fling open, and she

watched her father-in-law tumble down the stairs, landing at the bottom with a thud.

"Whoops," Hammons called out from above. "Did I do that?" Eventually, he descended the stairs. "All right!" he clapped. "Time to get this little party started." He laughed, stopping directly in front of Addison. "It looks like lover boy isn't doing too well, huh? That's quite a lot of blood we've got here," he said, kneeling. "Impressive. And look at you... You know, I'd forgotten how pretty you really are."

He taunted Addison. She recoiled. So, he took her hair in his hand, letting it slip through his fingertips. She backed away, but it only caused him to pull harder. "This pretty long blond hair. And my, my, my, those eyes. As blue as the sky, they are. Man! It's just too bad you had to turn out to be such a little whore," he said, pulling harder. "You do realize that if you'd just kept your legs closed that none of this would be happening, right?" Hammons made a clucking sound with his tongue and then shook his head. "Stand up," he said, lifting her by the hair. She had no choice, so she did as she was told. He studied her intently. "What a foolish, foolish girl you are for believing that this bastard could love you. He used you up and then tossed you aside just like everything else, didn't he?"

Addison refused to respond. She met his glare head on, until he backhanded her with seemingly every bit of strength he had. She staggered a bit, and then he really let loose on her, knocking her to the ground. He kicked her repeatedly. Somewhere around the third or fourth kick, Addison heard the shot fire off. She watched Hammons stagger. She saw the confusion on his face. As he reached for the gun at his waist, she lunged forward and sunk her teeth into his ankle, biting into it as hard as she could. He grabbed her head and tore at her hair as two more shots rang out in rapid succession. As though time had suddenly stopped, Addison watched in slow motion as the blood splattered across the room. It covered her. Hammons fell forward, half of him landing on top of her, the other half falling to the floor, bouncing as he hit the ground. She squirmed, trying to push him off. But it was useless. He was dead weight. He lay motionless, staring at her, a blank expression upon his face. The sound of her own screams was the last thing Addison recalled before she blacked out.

CHAPTER EIGHTEEN

William watched the flash of red and blue lights from the windows in the back of the ambulance. He kept asking about Addison, but no one was answering with anything definite. Everything was happening so fast. Teams of law enforcement had descended on the property, and medical personnel were shouting questions at him left and right, but the only thing he could think of was her. When he'd fired the shots and Hammons went down, Addison lost it. He didn't think she'd been hit, not until the screams started, and then she blacked out, and there was all the blood, so much blood that he couldn't tell where it was coming from. He'd been trying to help her as best he could—considering his injuries—trying to get her to respond when the cops had come storming in, weapons drawn.

He listened as the medics rattled off his vitals. They cut his clothes from his body and placed an oxygen mask over his face. He faded in and out while they inspected his various injuries. At some point, an officer began rattling off questions directed at him. William could barely breathe, and he sure as hell couldn't speak with that damned thing on his face, so he kept his gaze focused on the lights. *And his thoughts on her.*

"He keeps asking about the girl."

"The girl?"

The officer chuckled and took a step back. "You do know who this is, right?"

William watched the man as he considered him and then shook his head. "Should I?"

The medic smiled. "It's William Hartman, that gazillionaire from Austin—the one who's been all over the news. The one who got mixed up with that married woman."

"What's his status?" the officer demanded.

The EMT continued trying to run an IV but after a moment he paused and sighed. "Serious, if not critical. Likely has a collapsed lung. I suspect a head injury. A few broken bones... Non-responsive other than repetitively asking after the girl."

The officer nodded. "All right, I'll meet you guys at the hospital."

"Officer?" the medic called after him, his tone serious.

The man paused and then peered quizzically around the side of the door.

"The girl? How is she?"

William turned slowly, attempting to see the officer's expression, but they'd strapped him down and his head wouldn't budge.

"About the same," he said. "That asshole really did a number on them."

~

THAT NIGHT PATRICK HAD SPOTTED HIS MOTHER, WHO WAS severely hypothermic and as she often reminded him, not too far from death, walking along the side of the road. He pulled over, helped her into the Jeep, and drove them to the nearest house to call for help. He hadn't spoken to her since. He hadn't visited her in the hospital nor had he returned her calls. To tell the truth, at the moment, he wasn't quite sure whether he ever wanted to speak to her again. When all the facts came out, he'd just grown more and more furious at her for what she'd put his family through. He didn't know how he could possibly ever trust her again. His father had suffered a heart attack and spent one night in the hospital but seemed to be recovering well in his temporary apartment. Patrick had heard that Penny had visited him there a few times, but from what he gathered, his dad didn't seem ready to move back home anytime soon.

Michele was feeling better and had been staying with Patrick at his place since he'd had to care for the boys while Addison recovered. Thankfully, the boys seemed to be doing okay despite the circumstances. They were worried about Addison, of course, but luckily, they didn't really know all that much about what had taken place that night, other than their mother had gotten hurt. Michele had been a tremendous help with them, and they seemed to have taken a liking to having her around. Patrick took them to visit Addison daily. She was still in the hospital, learning to function on her own again. Having suffered broken ribs and a broken arm in addition to a head injury, he was told it could be weeks before she'd be well enough to take over with the children. Apparently, Hammons had succeeded in delivering quite a few blows to her head before Hartman could get a clear enough shot. The docs told Patrick that the headaches seemed to be improving. However, she still couldn't be exposed to much light and noise seemed to really bother her. She was always glad to see the kids, and although Patrick hated taking them to see their mother like that, he believed it was helping with her recovery, and the boys were always just as happy to see Addison, as she was to see them. They'd proudly decorated her room with flowers, pictures, and cards, which Michele had helped them make.

Patrick had mostly been able to work from home but was set to go back to work within the next few days, which he looked forward to. The only good thing to come out of any of this was that his family's situation had garnered so much attention lately that the higher-ups had decided not to transfer him after all, despite his and Michele's relationship.

Speaking of Michele, while he couldn't say exactly what the future might hold, he knew he wanted to be there for his daughter. He loved Michele in his own way and he figured he ought to give their relationship a shot, not only for the baby on its way, but also because Addison herself had so clearly moved on. It was probably time that he did the same.

~

ADDISON SHOOK HER HEAD AT THE NURSE'S INSISTENCE THAT she eat. She wasn't hungry, she assured her, but the nurse kept at it until Addison picked up the tray and flung it across the room. She hated behaving that way. It wasn't like her, and yet, she couldn't help herself. She was angry, and the pain was overwhelming. She didn't want to be in the hospital, confined to a bed, unable to do anything without help. She hadn't asked for any of this, and she certainly didn't deserve all of the pain she'd endured. *So why her?* All she wanted was to be home with her boys—not here—not in this condition where the nightmares always came and she was never quite sure whether she was dreaming or awake.

The boys came to visit daily, and that was the only sliver of the day she was truly herself. She masked the pain she was in, she smiled, and sometimes, she even laughed, but it wasn't the same. *Nothing was the same.*

She had a steady stream of visitors, but the nurses would only let them stay for a few minutes before kicking them out, telling them she needed her rest. Except for William, that is. They let William stay as long as he wanted. He'd wheel himself into her room and stay for hours, holding her hand, often times without speaking at all. He was better off than she was, having only suffered a few broken ribs, or so he'd said, a broken arm, and a collapsed lung. Addison didn't quite understand that because she'd watched Hammons beat William ten times worse than she herself had been beaten, or at least what she remembered of it anyway.

Jess visited, too. She'd been helping Patrick with the boys by taking them on fun outings and once to her house for a sleepover. She was intent on hearing all of the details of what had happened, causing Addison to snap because she just wasn't ready to go there. Not yet. Most of it had been reported in the news anyway, so she really didn't understand Jess's need to quiz her on the matter. But that was Jess; she'd always believed in talking things out. *It was best to process things*, she'd say. Still, Addison didn't see it that way. When it came to a lot of the situations in her life, she'd always found that silence was golden. And so, when Jess kept at it and didn't seem to get that she was in no condition to discuss any of it, Addison told her not to come back. Afterward, she felt terrible for it, but she hadn't been able to hold it in any longer. She did not want to talk about what had happened. *Why couldn't they get that?* There was only one person who seemed to understand her, and it scared her to think that she'd probably only end up hurting him too, in the long run. The doctors and the therapists told her that this kind of behavior was typical for head-injury patients. Anger, sudden outbursts and the inability to concentrate were all par for the course, they'd explained. Over and over. Apparently, memory loss was another 'completely normal byproduct.' *Lucky her.*

Sondra had visited almost every day and had even brought the baby up once. On one of her visits in an attempt to cheer Addison up, or something of the sort, she told her the story of the little guy's father. As it turned out, he was a very well-known and *very* married politician who visited Sondra and the baby often, but never promised more than that. Admittedly, Addison could now see how much the baby looked like him. Sondra joked about being head over heels in love with a man who would probably never love her back. Addison laughed when she told her she'd never wanted a happy-ever-after, anyways.

Only Sondra could say something like that and make it funny. She found herself grateful for Sondra's friendship. She never asked her to elaborate on what had happened, she never pressed for more. At least when she knew Addison couldn't give it. Other times were fair game. Sondra was one of those rare people in this word who were real. She never tried to be anything other than what she was, and Addison figured she could learn a thing or two from that. Eventually, on a later visit, she'd brought with her an offer that Addison couldn't quite push out of her mind. They both laughed over Addison being willing to listen to Sondra even so much as utter the word "offer" given all that had happened. But this one, as she'd later decide, didn't sound half bad. She could use a change; that much she knew. And the more she thought about it, the more she realized that, after everything she had been through, Sondra's idea was one of the few things that beckoned her to try, to keep going, no matter how much it hurt.

CHAPTER NINETEEN

William picked up his crutches and stared at his reflection in the mirror before hobbling toward Addison's room. They were getting ready to release him, even though he wasn't quite sure how he felt about it. He'd already bought himself a few extra days and could easily have paid for more, but something in Addison's demeanor told him that maybe he should go. The last thing he wanted to do was to leave her, but just because he was no longer considered a patient didn't mean he had to leave the hospital.

She wanted space, he would give it to her. She'd been through a lot. Hell, they'd all been through a lot, but the blatant truth was that it was his fault. Sure, what had happened to them at the hands of Scott Hammons wasn't exactly William's fault per se, but the fact was that being with a man like him would always make anyone he loved a target. If she chose a life with him, there would always be the possibility that something like this could happen again. He knew it was asking a lot. Men like him didn't get to live like everyone else. The lifestyle came with a lot of perks, sure, but it also came with an incredible price, too. It was a very different way to live, and the loss of anonymity alone was enough to make most people opt out once the curtain was pulled back, the truth revealed. He had chosen this life. It was what he knew, but to ask someone else to make that choice, to give up so much . . . well, it was a lot to ask. William knew Addison loved him; he knew that. But he also knew that she was as smart as they came, and so it had to be weighing on her mind whether or not *this* was really what she wanted, not just for her but for her children.

He knocked quietly on the door and entered the room to find her sitting up in bed, staring out the window. She didn't turn, but he could tell she knew he was there. Propping his crutches against the bed, he sat down and placed a hand on her thigh. When she turned, he saw the tears in her eyes. "Hey, hey, hey," he said softly. But this woman, the one staring back at him wasn't the Addison he knew.

"Come here," he said, taking her hands in his.

She wiped her eyes and stared at him, her expression blank.

"I heard you did really well in physical therapy today," he remarked. "They say with effort like that you'll be out of here in no time..."

"Yeah."

William traced I love you on her thigh with his finger in an attempt to lighten the mood. When she didn't say anything, he patted her leg. "So, what's up?"

Addison laid her head back against the bed and closed her eyes. "There's something I need to talk to you about."

He figured as much. "All right."

She opened her eyes and stared at his mouth. "Sondra made me an offer."

Wonderful. He frowned. "Another one, huh?"

She nodded.

"Well, you'd better get on with it," he said, hoping his sarcasm was clear. "I can't wait to hear this one."

"The agency wants to open in new markets, and they want to send me to do some of the upfront leg work," she said, not taking her eyes from his.

He wasn't surprised. Not in the least. He knew Sondra. He knew she was like him. Which was fine, normally. But not when it came to Addison. "Okay?"

"Well, I talked it over with Patrick, and he's given me permission to take the boys. So, I'm going to tell her yes."

He kept his expression neutral, even managing to raise his brow. "Is that so?"

"I'm . . . I'm guessing we'll leave within the next month or so," she told him. "Once I get back on my feet."

"I see," he said, pursing his lips. "I mean, if that's what you want to do, then I think it's a great idea."

"Really?" Addison asked. Eventually, she crossed her arms and cocked her head to the side.

William grinned and took aim. "Yeah, if that's what you want. But I'm going to go ahead and take a moment to call you out on your own bullshit."

She bit her lip.

"If you wanna go, that's great. I'm behind you one hundred percent; although, I think we both know why you're really doing this."

"Why?"

"You're running, Addison. You're scared and you're running, which is fine, but if you think I'm gonna let you off the hook, just like that, well, you've got another thing coming."

She looked away. "You're wrong. I'm not scared, and I'm not running."

William mirrored her demeanor, sighed, and called her bluff. "All right, then. Let me come with you," he said and then he paused and rubbed his jaw. "Where are we going, anyway?" he asked. "Somewhere warm, I hope."

"Come with me?" she said, shock written across her face. "Are you kidding? You can't come with me…"

He deadpanned. "The hell I can't."

She narrowed her eyes. She hadn't expected him to suggest that. "Your life is here. Your work is here."

"My life is with you," he corrected her. "My work can be anywhere I want it to be."

"But . . ." Addison exhaled. She looked away and rubbed at her temples.

"I'm the boss, remember? I can work from anywhere," he reminded her. He'd gotten her attention. Then he'd taken her chin in his hand, forcing her to look at him. "I also have the ability to fly where I want, when I want. Location and distance are non-issues in our relationship, Addison. So, if you want to call this off—if you want to run—you're going to have to do better than that because I'm not *him*. I'll fight for you every goddamned step of the way," he said, his tone harsh. "Keep that in mind, all right?"

Addison turned and stared out the window again, but she couldn't hide the smile on her face, hard as she tried.

William reached for her hand. "It's okay to be scared, you know. It comes with the territory."

"Are you scared?" she asked, quietly.

William inhaled and hesitated before speaking. "Am I scared? Hmmm, yeah, I guess you could say there are a few things that scare me."

She turned her head to face him. "Like what?"

He smiled. "Well, for starters, I'm scared of losing you. I'm scared that *this* . . . that my life is too much for you and that sooner or later you'll want to leave. I'm scared that maybe you already do."

"Is that it?"

"No— I'm scared that your children won't like me, because I have no idea what I'm doing in that department. I'm scared that you won't let me give you everything I have to give. But mostly, I'm scared that if it takes me the rest of my life, even if that's another hundred years or more that it *still* won't be *enough* time to show you how I feel about you."

Addison wiped the tears from her eyes with the back of her hand and offered up a slight smile. "I can understand that."

~

As Penny closed the front door behind the last of the members of the garden party committee, she exhaled a sigh of relief. She hadn't been certain which way it would go. These days, she wasn't certain of much. Sitting down at the bar, she put her head in her hands. After having just hosted a luncheon for thirty-five ladies, she was exhausted. Ever since that dreadful night at the lake, she'd been a mess. Her son was no longer speaking to her, and her husband wasn't too far off. Any communication they had was fairly selective these days, and he'd been spending all of his time at his apartment in the city. Addison refused to see her and even went as far as barring her from the hospital. Her friends were constantly asking how she was doing, and Penny was afraid that she'd only be able to keep up the front for so long. People were going to start talking, as if they weren't already.

She tried going through Patrick's mistress, but even she'd given Penny a run for her money. Penny had thought Addison was bad all these years; well, this woman put her to shame. Penny wasn't one to give up, and this woman was going to be the mother of her granddaughter, so she'd keep trying, if she had to. But admittedly, part of her wondered if that baby was her son's at all. If it were her, she'd be demanding a paternity test ASAP. She was going to have to talk to Patrick about that when and if he ever spoke to her again.

She'd heard from her husband that Addison had been released from the hospital and that she and the boys had been staying with that Hartman character. She was going to have to talk to Patrick about that, too. She couldn't see how her son could be okay with that situation. Not to mention the fact that her relationship with her grandsons would probably never be the same.

Penny had started seeing a therapist after the incident at the lake house, which had since, unfortunately, been put on the market. Penny hated to see that house go—she always had loved it so—but her husband hadn't given her a choice in the matter. Anyhow, at her husband's insistence, she started seeing this therapist, which she clearly didn't need, especially after he'd tried to diagnose her with something called NPD in addition to Post Traumatic Stress Disorder, which she was pretty sure he *was* right about. While she liked the guy and agreed with the PTSD theory, she vehemently denied having Narcissistic Personality Disorder. Dr. Brandt explained that she appeared to be a classic case. He went on to say that there was treatment for this sort of thing but it required first admitting there was a problem. Needless to say, she hadn't been back. Therapists were a dime a dozen, anyway; she explained that to her husband. She just needed a second opinion.

~

ABOUT SIX WEEKS AFTER SHE'D BEEN RELEASED FROM THE hospital, Addison met Jess for coffee at their usual spot. The weather was finally starting to warm up a bit, which may have been the reason the coffee shop didn't seem as busy as it usually did. As Addison placed her order, it suddenly took her by surprise just how much she was going to miss this. She considered how much their lives had changed since they'd first started meeting here, and she smiled to herself, thinking back on it all. She pictured the two of them meeting there as girlfriends in college before kids, before marriage, and then with babies in strollers, and then toddlers they couldn't contain, and suddenly, everything came rushing back to her. In many ways, it felt as though this were yet another one of the transitions that time often brought with it. But in others it felt like an ending of sorts. Or maybe it was just a beginning that hadn't quite happened yet. That's the thing about life and all of its ups and downs. Usually you don't quite know where it is you are, until you've arrived.

Addison stood in line watching Jess. She was bent over, writing in a notebook, and Addison couldn't help but notice how tired her friend looked. It made her feel bad that she'd been so wrapped up in her own problems lately that she hadn't even stopped to consider that her best friend might need an ear, too.

Jessica looked up, meeting Addison's eye, and suddenly her serious expression gave way to a smile.

Addison grabbed her coffee from the barista and made her way over to the table. They made idle chitchat for a bit before Addison leaned in close and narrowed her eyes. So . . ." she said. "How are you? I feel like we haven't actually talked about *you* for a while. And I really want to apologize for that, among other things."

Jess cocked her head. "I'm fine."

"Fine is a bullshit word," Addison said peering over her coffee.

Jessica waved her off. "Please. You know it's just more of the same for me."

"I'm sorry, Jess."

"Really—" she said, "There's no need to apologize."

"But there is. That day in the hospital . . . The way I acted was totally uncalled for," Addison argued. "I never should have talked to you that way, and I've regretted it ever since. I love you, Jess."

"Oh that," Jessica said with a fake laugh. "Come on. I knew you'd been through a lot, and I was pressing. I was the one who was out of line. Plus, I realize you didn't really mean any of it."

Addison inhaled and then sat up straighter. "How are you *really*, Jess? I can see that something's going on . . ."

Her friend looked away. "I'm fine," she swore. "I mean... the kids are driving me crazy, and I'm working on a new project that's been keeping me up... but enough about me—" She paused and then smiled. "I really did come here to hear about you. This time next week you're off, huh?"

"Project?" Addison said. "What sort of project? A PTA thing?"

Jess threw her head back and laughed. "No, it's not a PTA thing. Just something I've been working on. Writing, I mean. I'll tell you all about it, but first, I want to hear about you." She took a sip of her coffee and eyed Addison. "This time next week you'll be in Switzerland. How crazy is that?" Jess asked, her eyes widening.

"Pretty crazy."

"Speaking of which—how's everything going with Mr. Handsome?"

Addison grinned. "A little bit surreal."

Jess nodded. "I bet. So, what's the plan?"

"Well..." Addison started and then paused to glance at her phone. "First," she said, clicking her phone off. She looked up. "We're headed to Geneva, where we'll be for three to four months, and from there, it's looking like either St. Kitts or possibly somewhere in the Dominican—"

"Wow," Jess said. "The boys told me how excited they are. It seems like they're really looking forward to it…"

"Yeah. Partially, I think because Kelsey's coming. They just love her. She's the best nanny ever, I swear. But also because William is dead set on making it fun for them."

"And Patrick?"

Addison rubbed her neck. "Patrick seems to be doing okay with it all. And . . . I think that helps."

"It probably helps that he has his hands full with what's-her-name."

"You think?" Addison laughed. "But truthfully, if I felt that they weren't on board with the whole thing, I wouldn't be going. It's pretty amazing how much life can change in a year, you know?"

Jessica smiled. "I do know. And William? You evaded my question… How's all that going?"

"I did not."

Jess frowned. "You did…"

Addison hesitated before leaning in close and resting her elbows on the table. She placed her chin in her palm. "It's going—oh my God—beautifully. He's just—I don't know—everything I've ever wanted. It was rough after it all happened, you know. I mean I wasn't sure whether I was making the right decision, starting a relationship with such a complicated man, especially because it's all so different—being with him, I mean."

"I don't know what you mean," Jess interrupted. Her face lit up. "But go on…"

Addison sighed. "Then while I was recovering, I realized that I made the best decision of my life, besides having my children. These past few weeks have been incredibly hard and still, somehow beautiful at the same time. He lost a real friend in Carl and he's hurting."

"I can imagine."

"That and he's been dealing with his own recovery as well as mine, too."

"I'm sure he has a lot of help…"

Addison shrugged. "Still, it's been a lot, but he really took care of me, and I let him. I guess I just gave into it. It's crazy, but we've learned *so* much about each other in the past few weeks."

"Details… you know me…I want details…"

Addison shrugged again. "I don't know what to say—"

"Except?"

"Except, he's an addiction, and I just can't get enough."

"Damn, girl, you've got it bad," Jess smiled. "I told you from the beginning that you were in so much trouble with *that* one."

Addison blushed. "I know you did. And I am. But, you know, I think the key is to not completely lose myself the way I did in my marriage. It would be so easy to do it with *him*, too."

"I feel a but coming on…"

"But I won't let it happen, though. He either loves me for *me*, or he doesn't and that's it. I'm not giving up what I want any longer. And so far he seems to get that. I mean coming with me on this trip…that was all his idea. I thought he was crazy. I mean I still think he's crazy. But he really wanted it."

"I bet he did."

Addison didn't take the bait. "He's so smart about it all. The way he thinks . . . His business acumen . . . I mean… I never get tired of finding new things to love about him. It's funny because, well, obviously he's been ultra-successful, but he doesn't make me feel inferior about any of it."

Jess sipped her coffee. "How so?"

"He asks my opinion about things, and he listens. He doesn't shove opinions down my throat, either. He lets me come to my own conclusions about things. I don't know,"

Addison told her, looking away. "It's all just so different. And the boys . . . They really like him. He's so good with them. I mean *so* good."

"Sounds like it's everything you've ever wanted," Jess replied. She smiled after she'd said it but Addison could detect the sadness in her friend's eyes.

"It's a little scary though because I watch him with them, and I think about what a great father he'd make. I mean we haven't talked about it or anything... but I just don't think I want any more children."

"You might change your mind."

Addison shook her head. "I don't know. I'm not so sure."

Jess shifted and lowered her voice. "What about the other issues? How are you guys handling that? I can't imagine giving him what he needs is easy."

"Issues?"

Jess smiled. "You know, the kinky shit."

She raised her brow. "Oh, that..."

"I guess it's all normal to you now."

Addison furrowed her brow. "I don't know what normal is anymore."

Jess shook her coffee cup, stirring its contents. "And? What does that mean exactly?"

"And...I don't know.... we're kind of handling it our way. I give him what he needs, and somehow, he just senses what it is that I need. It's a pretty adventurous learning curve; I'll just say that. We're vanilla when we want to be, but there's not much that's off limits, and it's nice. It's refreshing."

Jess furrowed her brow and downed the last of her coffee. "You think you'll ever marry him?"

Addison snorted, choking on her coffee. "No. I don't think so. I'm not sure getting married again is in the cards for me. Right now, I'm just taking things one day at a time."

"Hmmm..."

"We've . . . Well, he's talked about it," Addison confessed. "He's mentioned it, but I keep saying no, and although he keeps asking and I keep saying no, I think he's content with that. I'm not going anywhere, and I don't think he is, either."

"Well, you're going *somewhere.*"

Addison leaned back and took her friend in. "I'm going to miss you so much, Jess. I'm gonna miss our little dates. Sure, we'll keep in touch, but it won't be the same."

"No. It won't."

Addison raised her cup and pointed it in her friend's direction. "I love you, Jess."

"Ditto," Jessica said.

Addison smiled and tilted her cup. "Here's to friendship, to *us*, and to going somewhere and nowhere all at the same time."

CHAPTER TWENTY

A note from the narrator:

One of my most favorite quotes says something about the fact that when you're in the middle of a story, it isn't a story at all; that only afterword does it begin to resemble something which makes any sense. I wholeheartedly agree, and as a reader, you should know that it took me a long time before Addison would agree to let me tell *her* story. Undoubtedly, it's understandable. I of all people get why she would be protective of her little love story. Nonetheless, if it were going to be told, and it had been—it wasn't long before it was splashed all over the gossip sites—she wanted it told as it was, as it had *actually* been, blemishes and all. But, before she finally agreed, of course, names had to be changed, and in order to get it just right, the way she wanted it, it had to be written and rewritten. Quite frankly, it required a lot of research and hours upon hours of interviews to make sure everything was factual—aside from the actual identities of those involved. That's the funny thing about stories, you know. What may be factual to one is almost certainly *never* factual to another. But, I digress.

Anyway, after I wrote and published the first part of this story, I was disappointed to hear so many of you say that you didn't like Addison—that you couldn't relate to her at all. When I heard that you'd called her selfish, it made me question my reasoning for telling her story in the first place. It's hard to hear those things about someone you care about so much. I mean, sure, a part of me could understand why you'd think that. For a good bit of time, Addison was pretty unlikeable, even to me. And I'll admit that in the beginning I was disappointed in her too, not only for doing what she did with William but also for being so blatantly honest and in your face about who she was and what it was she wanted, once she had.

Sure, she lied and she hid the affair upfront; and in doing so she let a lot of us down. And it's hard for many of us to understand her exact motives and why she would make the choices she did. But in writing this story and in knowing Addison, I can tell you it wasn't her intention to hurt anyone. What I learned from her is that love doesn't have an off-and-on switch. Sometimes it just hits you, and there's nothing much you can do about it. You have to go along for the ride and see where you end up. In addition, if you really knew her the way I do, then you'd know that she loved William from the beginning. She's always loved him. And I believe that when you love someone *that* much, it's hard to know what the right thing is because no matter what you decide, someone gets hurt.

But even I couldn't see that at first. All I could see were my own fears about my own life, which I was admittedly angry with her about revealing, by the way. I realize now how silly that all seems, looking back. But it took almost losing my best friend to really get it. If you stop and think about it, *how many of us are incapable of being truly brave when it comes to love?* We all tend to hide a little bit of who we are: the parts of ourselves we don't want anyone to see. Perhaps, it's because we think it's safer that way. What I realized though, is that, too, is a lie we buy into. One day, shortly after this revelation, it dawned on me, during one of my meetings with Addison in the coffee shop, not long after she'd been released from the hospital, that perhaps I didn't really do her story justice after all. Maybe there was more to the story than I was allowing myself to see. There almost always *is* more to the story, you know.

The truth is, I'm mostly just a bored housewife posing as a writer. But what I know for sure is that watching Addison's story unfold, gave me the courage to tell it. Seeing her follow her dreams—even if it meant hurting people she loved—gave me the strength to follow mine. Not because I'm a great writer or anything but because hers was a story worth telling. The thing about Addison that I think is so easy to hate—unless you love her, of course—is that she's different. She's bold, and she's courageous, and she goes after what she wants. That's an easy quality to despise in someone because there are a lot of people out there that don't. Take me, for example. I've been busy telling someone else's story—judging someone else's story—while hiding behind the facade I've created. On the outside, everyone thinks I'm fine. Everyone thinks I'm happy—when it isn't fine—and I'm not happy. On the surface, it was easy to tell myself that I was mad at her because of this or that. But that wasn't the whole truth.

You see, it wasn't until I sat down to write the continuation of her story that I really understood the half of it. It was then that I realized I hadn't been mad at Addison for what it was I thought she'd done. I was angry at her for becoming unapologetically more of who she was meant to be. When she revealed what she wanted, who she'd become at Seven and in her everyday life, that person was incidentally not who or what I wanted her to be. In turn, it forced me to confront my fears about whether or not I was willing to do the same in my own life. Maybe it takes a strong person, a person *like* Addison, I guess, to step out and shake things up. She's someone who is willing to put it all on the line for love, to show the rest of us that it's okay to do the same. All I know is that in the end, the strength she showed forced me to look at, to really see, the lies I'd been buying myself. Maybe someday, I'll be brave enough to tell my own story. Who knows, maybe someday, we all will.

You see—truth be told—I think that there's something about watching someone fumble, seeing them screw up, in all its glory that appeals to us, isn't there? It gives us a false sense of security, it tricks us into thinking we're superior, and some-times it even allows us to believe *we're* not so bad after all. From the outside looking in, it's probably easy to say what we would've done had we been in Addison's shoes—that *we* would, of course, always do the right thing. *But who really knows.* In the end, I think Addison did what was right for her. What I know for sure is that her effort to go after what she knew to be true, has in turn allowed me to realize my own truth. And I hope that after reading this you might think about yours. We all have secrets, even, and I would argue, *especially* those of us who appear to have it all together. In fact, I finally worked up the courage to sit down and write a whole book about mine. The thing is, you never know. *You really just never know.*

Thank you for reading,
Jess

EPILOGUE

Seven months later

Addison stared out the window, watching the lights twinkle in the distance as the plane slowly made its descent. *That had always been her favorite part of flying, the descent.* It was almost as though you were floating and then, BAM, at once, all of a sudden you were *there. You'd arrived.* Out of the corner of her eye, she could see Connor stirring a little, and as she looked over at the greatest parts of her life, she smiled a little. They were excited to make the trip home, to see their dad and meet their new baby sister, and she was excited for them. Breaking her reverie, William squeezed her hand a little, nodded in the boys' direction and then back at her. He leaned over, kissed her temple, and whispered in her ear that he was the luckiest man on the planet. She looked back at him and smiled. *God, she loved him.* Glancing down at their hands intertwined, the diamond on her left hand caught her eye. She smiled and nodded back, raised her eyebrows, and squeezed. William had only asked her to marry him half a dozen times in the time they'd been away, and each time she'd turned him down. It wasn't until he'd arranged a surprise trip for her and the boys, taking them back to Capri, Italy, where they'd first fallen in love, and knelt right there on that very same beach that she'd changed her answer to a maybe. It didn't really matter, though. *He knew he had her right where he wanted her, and she loved him even more for it.*

The five of them had had the time of their lives over the past seven months, exploring new places, taking it all in together, and finding more reasons to love one another by the day. The boys, aside from missing their dad—though they talked nearly every day and had visited back home twice for a week at a time—were the happiest she'd ever seen them. She couldn't help but think that maybe it was because she herself was finally happy. But now, it was time to stay home in Austin for a little while, to settle. William had purchased a home out on the lake, and Addison had agreed to give up her rental.

Later that day, as she entered the hospital corridors with the boys, it suddenly hit her that it wasn't all that long ago that she herself had spent time there. Maybe it was the sights and the smells that made it all come rushing back, she wasn't sure. The memories were fuzzy now; they had an aura about them, the nostalgic haze that memories sometimes get, and she couldn't help but think how it seemed like a lifetime ago that she'd been on the flip side of the coin. So much had changed since then. They'd stopped by the gift shop for balloons and flowers when Addison noticed "the book" sitting on the shelf, and suddenly her thoughts turned to Jessica and how much she couldn't wait to see her friend. She hadn't been angry about Jess telling her story so much as she'd been intrigued. She knew Jess needed the outlet, given her current situation, and so she gave it. Still, there was a lot they needed to discuss, and quite frankly, she'd been incredibly worried about her—in addition to guilt she felt for not being there when Jess had very clearly needed her. The twins interrupted her thoughts, tugging on her shorts, ushering her toward the cashier urgently, impatient to get upstairs and see the baby.

Addison couldn't help but smile at the flurry of pink balloons as she led the boys up to the room on the post-partum floor. She knocked, and when Patrick answered, she hugged and congratulated him and explained that she'd be down the hall in the waiting area. He grinned and thanked her as Michele's voice interrupted, asking her to stay. "We want you to meet her," she'd said. And suddenly, once again, she felt life as she knew it ever so slowly shift, as Patrick placed that little bundle of pink in her arms. She realized something then that she hadn't before. As she took it all in, watching her boys gently touching their sister's tiny hand and peering at her toes, everything changed. For the first time, she thought yes. *Just yes.* This was it.

She would finally say yes to William, not only because he wanted her to but because she wanted *this* for the both of them. Suddenly, all at once, she wanted everything.

∼

THREE DAYS LATER, ONCE THE MOVERS HAD JUST FINISHED UP, A courier delivered a handwritten letter. Addison studied the weight of the paper. She flipped it over in her hands and then brought it to her face and inhaled the perfumed scent. She traced her hands over the handwriting and Addison realized it could have only come from one person. She split the envelope carefully and pulled out the note. It was from Sondra and it read: *I have an offer...*

∼

ASHES. ASHES. WE ALL FALL DOWN. THE SONG RANG OVER AND over in Lydia Hammons head. She cupped her ears briefly and drove on. *That's the thing,* she thought. *No one pulls you aside and tells you what to do, how to act in these situations. No one prepares you for what it's like to pick up the remains of the man who raised you.* And yet, that's exactly what she'd just done. She walked right into that funeral home, as though she owned the place. She knew what they were thinking; she could see it written on their faces. Curious imbeciles, the lot of them. They wanted to see what the daughter of a psychopath looked like. Even if they tried to hide it. They weren't that good at hiding, not like her.

"Excuse me," the one with the bag in her hand said. She looked toward the far wall. They were lined up; five of them as though picking up ones dead father were a spectator event. "I'm afraid we haven't received payment... which we'll need before we release—"

"I get it," Lydia said, holding her hand up. "Someone has to pay."

The woman looked taken aback. Thankful, Lydia had spelled it out so she didn't have to. "Yes," she said, offering up a pen.

Lydia took the check from her pocket. "How much for the dead guy?" she joked. No one laughed.

"The total for cremation is $3,052.09."

Lydia raised her brow. "Wow," she told the woman. "They really stick it to you."

The funeral director pressed her lips together and then stared at the floor. "I'm very sorry for your loss."

Three thousand dollars, sorry? Lydia wondered. She handed the woman the check. It would bounce. But that was beside the point. She shrugged. "Someone has to pay though, right?"

The woman partially nodded and then handed her the bag. It was lighter than she'd expected. "Hi Daddy," Lydia said, holding the bag to her face. She was aware dead people couldn't talk back. But the people watching wanted a show and by god, that's what she would give them. She leaned forward and peered over the rim of the bag, looking down into it. "We have so much to discuss."

ASHES. ASHES. WE ALL FALL DOWN. *SOMEONE HAS TO PAY,* THE funeral director had said to her. Turns out, those were probably the most honest words that would ever leave that woman's mouth. Sure, she'd caused a scene back there. But she didn't feel bad about it. Not after they'd tried to guilt her into some elaborate affair, a celebration of her father's life to the tune of tens of thousands of dollars. "Just burn him," Lydia had said in the end. No need to exploit her grief any further.

"Don't worry Daddy. Someone's going to pay," she whispered, removing the box that held her father's remains. "And I know just where to start."

A NOTE FROM BRITNEY

Dear Reader,

I hope you enjoyed reading *Breaking Bedrock*. If you have a moment and you'd like to let me know what you thought, feel free to drop me an email (britney@britneyking.com).

Writing a book is an interesting adventure, but letting other people read it is like inviting them into your brain to rummage around. *This is what I like. This is the way I think.*

That feeling can be intense and interesting.

Thank you, again for reading my work. I don't have the backing or the advertising dollars of big publishing, but hopefully I have something better... readers who like the same kind of stories I do. If you are one of them please share with your friends and consider helping out by doing one (or all) of these quick things:

1. Drop me an email and let me know what you thought.

britney@britneyking.com

2. Visit my Review Page and write a 30 second review (even short ones make a big difference).

http://britneyking.com/aint-too-proud-to-beg-for-reviews/

Many readers don't realize what a difference reviews make but they make ALL the difference.

3. If you'd like to make sure you don't miss anything, to receive an email whenever I release a new title, sign up for my new release newsletter at:

https://britneyking.com/new-release-alerts/

Thanks for helping, and for reading *Breaking Bedrock*. It means a lot. Be sure to check out the second book in my latest series, *Beyond Bedrock* at the end of this book, as well as via your favorite retailer.

Britney King

Austin, Texas

December 2017

ABOUT THE AUTHOR

Britney King lives in Austin, Texas with her husband, children, two dogs, one ridiculous cat, and a partridge in a peach tree.

When she's not wrangling the things mentioned above, she writes psychological, domestic and romantic thrillers set in suburbia.

Without a doubt, she thinks connecting with readers is the best part of this gig. You can find Britney online here:

Email: britney@britneyking.com
Web: https://britneyking.com
Facebook: https://www.facebook.com/BritneyKingAuthor
Instagram: https://www.instagram.com/britneyking_/
Twitter: https://twitter.com/BritneyKing_
Goodreads: https://bit.ly/BritneyKingGoodreads
Pinterest: https://www.pinterest.com/britneyking_/

Happy reading.

ACKNOWLEDGMENTS

A big, BIG thank you to my friends and family for your support during the writing process and always for continually serving as personal cheerleaders along the way. Thanks for laughing with me—*or maybe it was at me*—either way. Nonetheless, I appreciate you being there.

A special thank you to Sebastian Kullas for so generously providing the cover art.

With extreme gratitude, I would like to acknowledge my beta readers. Thank you for your input each step of the way, for making this book what it is, and especially for incessantly bugging and motivating me to send you more.
Last, but certainly not least, I would like to thank the readers for every sweet note, for every review, for simply reading. You guys are everything. Thank you.

madman hell-bent on revenge. The series has been compared to Fatal Attraction, Single White Female, and Basic Instinct.

Around The Bend

Around The Bend, is a heart-pounding standalone which traces the journey of a well-to-do suburban housewife, and her life as it unravels, thanks to the secrets she keeps. If she were the only one with things she wanted to keep hidden, then maybe it wouldn't have turned out so bad. But she wasn't.

Somewhere With You | Book One
Anywhere With You | Book Two
The With You Series Box Set

The With You Series at its core is a deep love story about unlikely friends who travel the world; trying to find themselves, together and apart. Packed with drama and adventure along with a heavy dose of suspense, it has been compared to The Secret Life of Walter Mitty and Love, Rosie.

Series Praise

"Clever, intense and addictive."

"A surprising debut. Epic storytelling full of edge- of- your- seat suspense."

"Unputdownable."

"Hypnotic and breathtakingly romantic."

"Bold and in your face from the get-go."

"A twisty and edgy page-turner. The perfect psychological thriller."

"I read this novel in one sitting, captivated by the words on the page. The suspense was startling and well-done."

"Dark and complex."

"Exhilarating and suspenseful."

"A fascinating tale of marriage, secrets, and deception."

"Fast-paced and thrilling."

∾

In this dark and compulsive novel somewhere along the lines of *Single White Female* meets *Basic Instinct* comes a thrilling, addictively suspenseful, and haunting story that grabs the reader, and holds them captive until the very end. For fans of psychological thrillers, suspense, and the forbidden, *Beyond Bedrock* hands us a deceptively scary tale.

"She was the worst kind of evil. And I opened the door and watched her walk right on into our lives."

A story of obsession. A story about fatal attraction.

Addison and William Hartman's once tumultuous affair is mostly a thing of the past. These days it seems they have it all--that the world is literally at their fingertips.

Settled into a marriage that is anything but normal, it appears they have the give and take in the bag. That is until Addison makes a fatal mistake. When Lydia Hammons enters their lives it isn't because she needs a job. It's because she wants everything Addison has worked so hard to build, and she's hell-bent on having it--no matter the cost.

Just when it seems that their strength together will overcome any obstacle, fate--or perhaps something more sinister--conspires to see that their worst fears come true.

BEYOND BEDROCK

BRITNEY KING

COPYRIGHT

Hot Banana Press

Front Cover Design by Lisa Wilson

Back Cover Design by Britney King

Cover Image by Sebastian Kullas

Copy Editing by TW Manuscript Services

Proofread by Proofreading by the Page

First Edition: 2015

ISBN: 978-0-9892184-9-8 (Paperback)

ISBN: 978-0-9892184-3-6 (All E-Books)

britneyking.com

To the crazies.
For without the experience of
dealing with you—
this story could not have been written.

PROLOGUE

9:03 AM

Dearest William,

Schizoid personality disorder. This is the official diagnosis. It's amazing! They think they can just label a person using three words and that's who they are. Well, let me tell you. THEY are wrong. They think a piece of paper gives them the right to tell me who and what I am. THEY ARE THE CRAZY ONES! I am not those three words. I am a whole lot more than that. I am a person and I am in love with you.

This morning, I picked out a light blue top and jeans to wear. For you. For this occasion. To match your eyes, but also because blue signifies loyalty and honesty, and this is why I write. Because I will show them, and I will show you, that I am more than a label.

It wasn't easy at first. When I began writing to you in here. Honestly, I had no idea where it would take me. I simply picked up my pen, set it down, and thought of you—of what I wanted to say and the best way to say it.

It's been several weeks now, and I can feel things winding down. I believe this chapter is coming to an end. And by end, I mean my time in this place.

PROLOGUE

This will likely be my final chapter to you and every writer knows it's important to go out with a bang. As for what comes after, I do not know.

Because that's the thing, my love. Something always comes after. Bangs don't just occur, people just don't go down, and that's the end of it, you know. Someone has to pay. That is a true ending.

Alas, as I ponder how this part of our story will end, I realize endings are never truly endings and this brings me great comfort. It is important to get this right. I know this deep down in my bones and so I do the work. It's important, this much I know. And so, I balance the tray on my lap, consider my plan for a moment, and then place the notebook on top of it. I pause and consider how much to tell you, here and now, before we are finally together again, and so I simply stare out the window and think of your eyes.

As I watch the trees swaying in the wind, I think about the breeze and what it would feel like across my skin. If I had to guess, I'd say a lot like your lips.
Through the double-plated glass windows, I swear I can almost hear the birds chirping, and I think of you and the sound of your voice calling my name. It is then I realize I want my work and my time in here to mean something. That it has to.

It is also then that I truly understand the significance of her visits. This isn't just about her. It isn't about her getting the facts—or even the story.
It is about our story. It's about the story of our love. And then it hit me….
Who better to tell our story than me? It was then I decide what this all means.

This was never about her at all.
It was about us.
You and me.

This is our story and it has been my love letter to you.
In the spirit of the colors I'm wearing, and since we're being honest here, I want you to know I have written these letters to you. I have told our story in hopes you might come to understand the depth and the expansiveness of my love for you. So, by the time we are together again, in just a matter of hours now, you will see things differently.

I don't know how or why things got so mucked up, William. I don't. I only know that I am in here and you are out there. I know you have been confused about our feelings for one another. And I also realize this, our story, my work in progress, will fix it all.

Today, as I write this, I am unlike the birds I can so faintly make out chirping just beyond. I am locked away here on a 5150 involuntary psych hold, which was extended from seventy-two hours to fourteen days. Tomorrow there is to be a hearing.

But for the past thirteen days now, I've been locked in a cage, living as an animal, essentially—and likely, I understand at your doing.
Not because I've done anything wrong—but because you have friends in high places.

How could such a thing as sweet and pure as love be wrong, anyway, William?
Riddle me that.

But the good news is... I know it won't be long now.

They can't keep me locked in here forever.

For one, I have a plan. I'm sure you of all people understand that. And William, my William, if there is anything you should know, it is that I am not angry with you. There's not one ounce of bitterness in me toward you—only love. Always, only love. I want to be angry. Sure I do. But how could I be angry with someone whose love for me is so vast and so true that he has to keep me locked up just so he has me all to himself?

It was brilliant, honestly. And so very you, William. Just like the blue shirt I wear, you're loyal.

Not just to me, to your wife as well. I understand that now. Even if I don't necessarily like it... I understand.

You're sending me a message.

Because underneath all of that loyalty, like the shirt I wear, you're blue. The message you send is loud and clear—you want me as badly as I want you. I'm good at sensing these things. I always have been. But this doesn't mean it's easy, William. True love never is though, is it?

I do get upset from time to time and I do things. Bad things. Necessary things. Things I will tell you about someday soon— when we are together. It's just a matter of time as I help you to understand. And I will do that in my writing. It's the only way now. I will trade her. My story—our story—will be my letters to you, and they will set the record straight. It will be like sending messages in a bottle and we will get it right.

Soon enough, though, I will be like the birds I hear in the distance, free from this cage. Free to express my love for you in all the ways that count.
Until then, it should bring us both great comfort to know, that in my mind, I am like the birds now—here, in this moment.

And this story, the story of us, is my song to you.

Kisses,

L

P.S. I wrote you a poem:

One can only deny the truth
for so long.
Forever, maybe.
But forever has nothing on
the way I feel about you.

CHAPTER ONE

Ten Days Prior

As she sat at her kitchen table with the notes laid out before her, she considered how today's meeting with Lydia had gone as well as one might have expected.

Knowing there was only one vice left these days she could rely on, she picked up the coffee she'd poured. *It was still too hot* .She placed her lips to the cup and blew into the mug. She took a sip knowing it would burn her. *Just the way Lydia Hammons would.* If she let her. *She had to be careful.* She sat that way for a while staring out the window. *Waiting. So much of their lives amounted to nothing more than waiting these days.*

Even still, she wasn't sure she could keep going. She only knew she had to. She was tired. Already, their meetings had taken a toll on her, given all she'd been through. She understood all too well trying to get this story might kill her.

Eventually, she gave up on waiting for the fix she so desperately needed to cool, and set the cup down, then turned her attention back to the letter. *Coffee, life, everything would have to wait.*

As she turned the pages over, she let the words replay in her mind. She'd known Lydia to be crazy—that was no secret. But she hadn't exactly predicted that she'd be so cunning. Definitely, not this clever.

She sighed, pushed the note away and picked up the coffee once again. What was laid out before her was hard to read and even more difficult to make sense of. But if there was an answer to be found that would save the people she loved, a plan, *anything*—a rhyme or reason to it all, it was she who would find it. *She had to.* She was on a mission.

She would pull herself together.

She would fix this.

She would get inside the mind of Lydia Hammons.

Even if it killed her.

She was determined.

And so she finished her coffee, and she read.

The Story of Us.
By Lydia H.

I knew I loved him from the first moment I saw him. I wore black as sure and as dark as night. It wasn't like you'd think… He didn't smile and take my hand the way I imagined. Our coming together wasn't like that at all. It was an ordinary morning, early spring, the sun bright and yet still further away than one knew it soon would be. Our love would burn just the same. Plus, everything shifts eventually. *Everything.*

Speaking of love, it wasn't supposed to happen like this. I didn't believe in love at first sight, at least not *before*. Now, I do. I can still recall it as though it happened just yesterday. I was brushing my teeth—half-listening to the morning news and half dreading going to the office. I brushed harder and watched the blood drip onto the porcelain as the crushing weight of the anxiety set in. I felt the familiar buzz; the low hum of noise that always precedes a full-blown panic attack. And then, all at once, I heard his voice and something inside me shook and shifted in the world. He was what I'd been waiting for. And when I heard that familiar voice, *I knew.* As he spoke, the buzzing stopped and there was clarity and crispness like I'd never known. At once, my vision for the future was focused and sharp.

Sure, I knew his name, who wouldn't, given all that had happened? I'd even made plans for us to meet. I just hadn't acted on them yet. I'd avoided him and anything even closely resembling what had once been—just like I avoided germs and crowds full of people. Crowds of people are overwhelming, (not to mention germ-infested) they're intimidating, foreign, and unknowing.

And until that moment, so had been William Hartman.

I spat blood into the sink and dropped the toothbrush onto the counter like the omen that it was. Then I turned my full attention back to the television where it belonged and wondered how it was possible anything on this earth could be so utterly perfect. I wasn't supposed to feel this way. I wasn't supposed to feel that sort of attraction. Given what he'd taken from me. But there he stood, in his crisp white shirt, suit, and tie, all of him—filling up so much space. As he spoke, he touched his tie and sucked the air right out of the room, and with it, the air from my lungs, and it was astonishing. One movement on his part and he suddenly set everything right in my world, and I wondered, *why now?* I remember that he was speaking on the Gleason merger, and I knew then we would become close. I knew then it was meant to be. I didn't know when or how, but I knew I'd find a way. My father taught me that 'where there's a will, there's a way!'—one of the few good things he'd ever imparted upon me—if we're being honest here, and we are.

I watched him finish the interview, and I no longer felt panicked or unease. I felt lighter and thinner.

Just like the black I wore.

I had a purpose now.

And that purpose was meeting him.

~

Her mood was red hot like the shirt she wore. On the day of their first visit, Lydia knew she was on fire. She'd ace this thing. She smiled and considered how long it had been since they'd last seen one another. *Too long,* she thought, picking at a faded thread, which hung from the borrowed shirt she wore. She smoothed the shirt across her sunken belly. Then she touched the thread, smiled, and caught the end of it. Lydia twirled it between her thumb and forefinger, watching as it unraveled—not unlike she herself had done. She pulled a little more and marveled at the irony of it all. *That's how it happens.* One teensy snag and suddenly, a pull this way or that way, and suddenly it becomes a whole other matter altogether. It amused her a great deal that one simple analogy pretty much summed up the entirety of her life. But that was a story for another day.

For now, she'd decided none of that was really very important anymore—for she'd gained what she'd been after —finally. A visitor!

It wasn't polite to withhold information, she knew. But it was smart. That's why Lydia decided to wait her out. She studied the thread she'd wrapped around her pinky and pulled tighter until her finger went from pink to purple to a beautiful shade of blue. Still, she pulled tighter. *She always had liked that shade of blue.*

Somewhere far off, she heard an unknown tune hummed, and she attempted to match it with the whirl of the ceiling fan above. She turned her ear ever so slightly toward the music, but the one thing she didn't do was look at the woman adjacent to her. She didn't need to. It was enough she felt the woman's gaze burning into her skin and looking up was unnecessary in times like these. *She was on fire.* She knew who the woman was and why she'd come and the rest was history.

Lydia cleared her throat and pulled tighter at the string. Later, she would come to realize that such a thing was her ticket. For now, she had work to do, so she released the thread just a little and spoke slowly without looking up. "I know why you're here," she said, losing at her own game. She shrugged. "You want answers… I get it. But I'm only going to agree to tell you my side of the story, which is what you want, isn't it—if you let me do the telling. I've worked it out already, and I've decided I'm going to go ahead and let you in —in order to share our story. His and mine, that is. But first, you should know, despite any preconceptions you might have, that this is about love. What I share with you is the truth as I know it, and I won't allow you or anyone else to deny me that."

The woman glanced at her expensive, over-priced shoes and then looked up at her.

Lydia smiled. "And if we are going to do this—and it seems we are, or you wouldn't be here, then we're either going to do it my way… or not at all."

"What does that mean Lydia?"

"It means that I will teach you the rules of the game, and you will listen. We will play together. Because only then will you understand, there are many sides to the truth. And no one wins a game of this kind. Not really. "

The woman exhaled slowly. *Already, she was listening.* "What makes you think I want to play your games?" She narrowed her eyes. "Haven't you considered that I've had enough? That maybe we all have…"

"You want the story. I know you do," Lydia said, cocking her head. "Otherwise you wouldn't be here."

Lydia watched as the woman stood and walked to the door, opening it hesitantly. She turned and paused just inside the frame. "I want answers; you're right about that much, at least," she said looking over her shoulder. "But you see, it takes two people to play a game, Lydia. And only one of us here is playing," she added, and then she smiled.

It was a pleasant smile. The kind that welcomed one in and invited them to stay awhile. Paradoxically, Lydia shook her head. "That's where you are wrong."

$\sim$

1:33 PM

Dear William,

Today marks my second day here and the first visit from her.

I have already decided that I will help her.

But she doesn't know that yet.

I will tell her what she wants to hear.

And maybe a few things she doesn't.

I think that in order to truly help her—to help us all; I have to take it back to the beginning. When we were all happy.

I see a pattern evolving here. I think you can see it, too. This is my specialty—seeing patterns—finding similarities. It is one reason you have come to love me, as I know you do. But then, you probably already know this. It was my knack for seeing the possibility even back then, on that very first day as I watched you on the news. I listened to your words ring aloud in my head, and from that, I understand the magnificence of timing and the reason it all played out just like magic.

Ironically, though, and sadly to her detriment, it would be your wife who loved me first.

And if it is any consolation, I will tell you this—in a perfect world, my dreams sometimes still include Addison. There are days I picture us as one big happy family. Of course, you love me more (and will always) because your love for me is in direct proportion to my love for you. Unlike Addison, my feelings for you are so wide and so deep that few people aside from the two of us can grasp what exactly it is that means. Or the lengths we would go to for one another. Just like what you did by placing me in here. It's extreme, but that's us, William. Always has been, always will be.

Also, since I'm wearing blue like your eyes and well because blue signifies honesty, I have to admit it's only on the good days that I imagine Addison being a part of our plan. Most days, I face the unfortunate reality of the situation (even more so now that I'm in here!) I know as long as she's in the picture, the more I realize she will only ever come between us. *Oh, how she likes to get in the way.* She makes you upset, William.

She provokes you and changes your mood. She sucks your energy away. She takes everything. She does the same to me. It's her fault the highs are so high and the lows are much too low.

Addison is what I like to call black magic. She does things to people. I know… I've seen it firsthand.

It happened the first time I ever met her.

Which, as hard as it is to believe, was six months ago now.

I guess it is as they say, time flies when you're having fun.

And I like to think we are.

Kisses,

L

P.S. I wrote another poem for you. I hope you like it.

There are so many parts and pieces
to the both of us.
Just think—
Of what we might amount to
if we put them all together.

～

On the second visit, Lydia showed up prepared. She wore a green sweater to match the plants she tended and to signify harmony. *Also growth.* That's what this visit was to be about. *Everything had a purpose.* Lydia watched as her opponent picked up the papers before her and studied them.

For now, they were enemies—but it wouldn't always be this way. Soon, there would be harmony between them as sure as the color green she wore.

Lydia studied the intricacies of the hardened expression the woman wore as she read the words that had been carefully crafted just for her. Well, for William truthfully—but she couldn't—or rather *shouldn't* say as much now. Lydia noticed the way her opponents nose curved a little, clearly broken once, a long time ago. She noted the way her eyebrows were meticulously over groomed. Maybe Lydia would do this to her own. *Like the color green one wore to blend in.* These were the little nuances she'd come to know here and there. Soon enough she would memorize by heart. That's where she'd write them, tuck them away for safekeeping.

Understanding the art of war, Lydia spoke first. "We're going to write the story together."

The woman studied the papers before her and drew a long breath. "Is that so?"

Lydia understood the woman needed her more than she wanted to admit.

They always did.

Things may have looked grim on her side of the table from where the other woman sat, but Lydia knew that everything would work out just as it should.

She would pull herself together.

She would fix this.

She would make everything right again.

Even if it killed her.

Or more likely, someone else.

And on that day, for the record, she wore green, just like envy.

∾

Learn more at: britneyking.com